Nosebleeds From Washington Heights

By

Gary Alexander Azerier

authorHOUSE™

1663 LIBERTY DRIVE, SUITE 200
BLOOMINGTON, INDIANA 47403
(800) 839-8640
WWW.AUTHORHOUSE.COM

First published by AuthorHouse 6/16/2006

ISBN: 1-4208-2053-2 (sc)

Library of Congress Control Number: 2004195264

Printed in the United States of America
Bloomington, Indiana

This book is printed on acid-free paper.

Acknowledgments

I should like to acknowledge all of my good friends who took the time to read these pieces as I recklessly sent them out, and who generously gave of their time, critical faculties, and candid opinions to offer encouragement and suggestions. Without their feedback, there would have been little reason to recreate these tales.

A special thank you, also, to Albert Wahnon who taught me how to decode Ovaltine messages without Captain Midnight's decoder when I was nine years old, taught me more, now, about skillful editing than I ever learned in formal English courses, and who was more than generous in sharing his time and professional expertise. It isn't easy to find a hero at my age. But my aunt Rose found him years ago.

And, to one of the best-loved men in New York, who feeds the hungry soul and spirit in this city with his warmth and goodness, Jimmy Neary.

Dedication

This collection of stories is dedicated to Betty and Mitchell, my mother and father, and my loving wife Rose Ann, without whose ear and encouragement, there would be no book.

Table of Contents

Foreword

In 1932, the beautiful George Washington Bridge was completed to span the Hudson River between Manhattan and Fort Lee, New Jersey. It graced the landscape of Washington Heights and lent an air of dignity and prestige to the clean and quiet neighborhoods that came together to form this upper stretch of Manhattan. The Heights boundaries were pretty much marked familiarly by Columbia Presbyterian Hospital, known informally as "Medical Center" on 168th Street and Broadway, to the south; the new and exclusive housing project Castle Village on the northern side of the bridge, beyond which lay the communities of Dyckman and Inwood; the Hudson River to the west, beyond which lay New Jersey; and the East River to the east (beyond which lay the Bronx). The neighborhood had elementary schools, P.S. 173, 187, 189, and 132, Junior High School 115, and George Washington High School. The main thoroughfare running north to south and cutting through the neighborhood was Broadway. It was, along with 181st Street—which ran west to east—a major shopping hub. Movie theaters, entertainment centers for all, included the first-run RKO Coliseum on 181st and Broadway and Loews 175th Street, also on Broadway. Second-run cinemas were the Lane, the Gem and farther east, the Empress, all on 181st Street. A little theater called The Heights, on Wadsworth Avenue, featured foreign and esoteric art films. The streets ran from Haven Avenue along the Hudson, to Cabrini Boulevard, Pinehurst Avenue, Fort Washington Avenue, where the 5th Avenue buses ran, Broadway, Wadsworth Avenue, Saint Nicholas Avenue, Audubon Avenue, and finally, Amsterdam Avenue. The area subway was primarily the 8th Avenue IND or Independent line with local stops being 168th Street, 175th Street, 181st Street and 190th Street, and the Broadway 7th Avenue line which stopped at 168th Street, 181st Street, and 191st Street, farther to the east. And there were parks, the most notable of which was, and still is, Fort Tryon Park, which houses the Cloisters at around 197th Street, and farther to the south, the little J. Hood Wright Park in the 170s, between Haven and Fort Washington Avenues.

Much has changed over the years. But for many years and for what may have seemed a select group of people, the neighborhood was a clean, cheery, fresh place in which to live, raise, and grow future citizens. It was a place in which to play, learn, make friends, and from which to venture forth. In those days of the 1940s and 50s, the air seemed clearer, the sky bluer, the streets cleaner, the sunshine brighter.

It is a darker place now; more confused and crowded. There is a lightness that is gone. It has the aura of desperation, not quiet. And if one wishes to visit that sunnier, bluer, and fresher place that the Heights once most certainly was, one has only memories to summon and recollections to visit.

George Washington Bridge, New York.

SPRING

Ben Borden

In the old days, when the house was young, her tenants were young, and come to think of it, the neighborhood was young. Change was on hold; frozen by catastrophic events. It was as if world affairs had created a climate in which it was too dangerous for major changes to take place at home; too risky. Change was taking place elsewhere; many of us were watching, remaining still, holding our breath. People held onto what they had. They didn't seem to age. Lives were on hold. We waited to see what the outcome of the war would be. Who would come home; who wouldn't.

Of course, people got older, but not so as you could notice. And oddly, no one died in the building during those years. But there were two gold stars on the flag that covered the wall next to the elevator. The two stars indicated two sons of the building who were killed in action overseas. You couldn't stand by the elevator and not see them.

There used to be a pretty little electric fireplace in the lobby that cast a red glow through large, dull chunks of colored glass. Its light had long gone out and it was dark.

The building had had a canopy. That too was long gone, as was the huge, majestic tapestry that graced the lobby. The telephone booth between stairwells was filled with rolls of rubber mats when the public telephone was removed, and after the war, the manually operated elevator was replaced by a self-service unit, exciting at first but never to compare with the class of the manned car, the sound of her gate opening and closing.

But for all of these superficial alterations, hardly anyone moved into the building. No one moved out. The war was on. No one was going anywhere. And everyone seemed to know everyone else. There were few strangers. It was a comfortable place.

Ruth Kruger, a nice, quiet, and attractive brunette who was always dressed elegantly, liked to hand me a dime occasionally. She would merely stop, rummage in her purse and, handing me the dime, for no reason, say: "Here." She had been engaged to one of the boys who was killed. Years later, my father befriended a man who became his best friend, who had borne the loss of a son during the war. My father learned quite casually one day, when his friend asked if we ever knew Ruth Kruger, that it was the man's son who had been Ruth's fiancé. It was his gold star we had been looking at all those years. Connections. Invisible threads.

The people next door to us were in close enough proximity to sport the titles of uncle and aunt. Otherwise they were Millie and Ben Borden. Millie and Ben lived in a two-room apartment like ours but had no children, so their place had a different climate. It was neat, tidy, if not sterile. On Millie's lovely coffee table was an oval china candy dish with a very delicate pattern. I was always offered a piece of candy from it. It was decidedly adult. It was not chocolaty; there were no jellies or marmalades or fruit-filled sweets. These offerings were more like mints, butterscotch, sugary, dull. It was candy of the worst variety I ever tasted. I never asked for a second piece and was always disappointed when Millie, on subsequent visits, lifted the china lid once again to reveal the same selection. This was the major treat, the only offering, the sole diversion in Millie and Ben's apartment.

Many a pleasant Sunday afternoon would find Millie and Ben strolling in the park or sitting on one of the many park benches. If a chill in the air called for it, Millie wore a fox stole, which fascinated me because the fox's face on it was still intact. It rivaled the candies for amusement. Millie was rarely hatless on these Sunday outings, wearing hats too complicated to describe.

Ben was always immaculately clad. His three-piece suits were perfectly fitted, neatly and sharply pressed, and of fine worsted wool. He was never seen outdoors without a hat. His hair was quite thin and he wore a crisply-turned-down gray fedora which he tilted at a rakish angle. And he sported a pencil-thin mustache. Ben could be described as dapper.

The Sunday meetings in the park were light and pleasant with a jovial air, sometimes terminating in a walk to one of our neighborhood bakeries for cakes which we might all later share over coffee (or milk), served on Millie's delicate china, on her coffee table. These Sunday afternoons were agreeable enough so that I often wished we might repeat the getting together at some future time during the week. Tuesday, however, was out of the question. Tuesday was Ben's night out with the boys.

There were many occasions when something or another arose on a Tuesday. My father would ring the Borden's bell. "No. We'd love to. But it's Ben's night out with…the boys."

It became somewhat of a joke and we never really knew what transpired during these "nights out." Nor did we ever get to see any of "the boys."

After the war, the changes that had been on hold began to take effect. It was like a sleeping giant beginning to stir. Some of the men came home. People purchased cars. Apartment dwellers purchased homes in New Jersey and moved away. New tenants moved into the building. The fireplace remained still. Some people died. And Millie, Millie began to change.

It started with her knocking on the wall. Incessant scales and piano practicing may have played a part in precipitating her response, but it escalated. Millie began to rap on the wall at the slightest noises. Every sound became a major disturbance that elicited from her a surge of pounding. And often my mother responded in kind. Soon we stopped talking to one another and glances when passing on the street were averted.

At first, Ben was apologetic, tried to explain, mollify, mediate. Nothing seemed to work and the situation became worse. Exacerbated by Millie's encroaching breakdown and perhaps by my conscientious practicing, we all avoided one another, Millie buried her head in the folds of her coat collar, took to the stairs if others were in the vicinity of the elevator, and even amiable, genial Ben stopped talking to us and avoided contact.

There were uncomfortable moments which were spent with Ben while awaiting the arrival of the elevator, riding with him in its enclosed space, or traversing our hallway together. But he was never anywhere to be seen in the building on Tuesday; boys' night out.

My father came home one night after a late meeting downtown at his office. It was on a Tuesday. He had been passing a Bickford's Cafeteria on Sixth Avenue when he happened to peer inside. There, he told us, sitting dressed immaculately, over a newspaper and coffee was Ben Borden. It was too late to have been early, too early to have been late. Had his night out been cancelled?

Only two weeks later, after years of tradition and mystery, my father had occasion to pass the Bickford's again, on a Tuesday night. Once more, the hour was late. He stopped at the window and scanned the interior. There in the back, sitting by himself, over a crumbling bran muffin and coffee, legs crossed as he read his paper, was Ben Borden. It was Boy's Night Out.

"ME, BEN, MOM, MILLIE AND FRIEND"

Miles

They thought they knew all there was to know. They thought they knew almost everyone worth knowing. They couldn't yet be fully aware of it, but to a large extent the perfection of their youth was beginning to flower: the vigor, the good health, the vital confidence as yet unjustifiable, the arrogance unfounded. But to paraphrase Thomas Wolfe, with whose *Web and the Rock* many of our classmates walked about for the months it took them to read the tome, they were the lords of life. They were plunging into their twenties, the threshold of adulthood, and they were the lords of life.

That year in graduate school saw a definitive dilution of academia, as well as of interesting and lively characters. I did befriend, for only a brief interval, a thoughtful and perceptive young man. He was older than I and seemed to have already suffered a sampling of what the cruel side of life had in store. He had been in the merchant marine and told of an old salt whom he recalled jawing with on the bridge as he was being relieved of his watch. The old sailor said to him: "You know, lad, there's only one thing you have that I don't have...and that's your youth. And that will soon be gone." Perry said its truthful ring gave him the chills and it was something he hadn't forgotten.

At the party, Perry had invited me to, I encountered the usual suspects, as students' panache preceded their flaunted forms. It was difficult to know whether conversations on essence preceded those on existence, or whether those on existence preceded those on essence. It made no difference, of course, but was taken seriously by those participating. Rye and gingers grew flat, CC and sodas got warm, as ice melted. The room grew smokier as introductions going nowhere persisted. The evening dissolved.

There were no fresh nor pretty faces that night, so I hacked a path through the crowd to the door. It was open, and beyond the exit's bottleneck, the yawning hallway gaped hollow and depressing. It was there, at this social bottleneck, that I ran into Manny Dunzler. I hadn't seen Dunzler since junior high school in Washington Heights, and we had advanced, apparently by a neighborhood or two and several years. Hopefully, we had also matured somewhat. Dunzler was likeable enough and offered a genuine smile as we shook hands and did a quick catching up. But he had initiated a pointless incident years ago for which I detested him. From the warmth of his greeting, it seemed as if he had forgotten all about it, about as justifiably as when he precipitated it. But I had not forgotten.

I had been on my way back to school for the afternoon session after lunching alone on 181st Street, at the Horn & Hardart Automat. From across the street, I heard a yell. It was Manny Dunzler and two of his friends. Although we were not fast friends, I stopped to wait. One of Dunzler's pals grabbed me from behind and Dunzler, without provocation, punched me in the gut. I struggled uselessly and glowered at him. Before his buddy would let me go, Dunzler extended his hand in friendship.

"Hey," he said, "I'm really sorry. You ok? If he lets go, you wanna shake?" And here he gestured with his extended hand. It made no sense, but I didn't seem to have much choice, and in view of being outnumbered, it seemed to be a way of cutting my losses.

"Ok," I said. And the boy behind me loosened his hold around my arms. Dunzler smiled. I shook his hand. He tightened his grip and swiped me in the face with his fist. He took a few skipping steps backward and, with his cohorts, ran away as I felt the warm trickle of blood from my nose. I never forgot Dunzler's leering face and my indignity at having been so badly duped. I had seen him in hallways and staging areas for the next few months spent at JHS 115, but our unresolved rancor was never addressed. Whatever may have instigated the incident remained a mystery which seemed eventually to dissolve, but, like after much evaporation, left a residue.

I was saying good-bye to Dunzler, nice having run into him and all, when a tall, lean, redheaded young man, a latecomer, stepped into the apartment. The guy looked more than familiar, although I had not seen him in at least a dozen years. He appeared handsome and distinguished in his dark overcoat, as well as successful. Holy cow! It was old Zack Miles. They called him Miles in the old neighborhood. His real name was Milowitz.

"Say," I said to him as he looked, perplexed, at me, "aren't you Zack Miles?" For years I thought his first name was actually Miles. It was only later that I learned his first name was Zack, and only later still that his real last name was Milowitz. I introduced myself and complimented my name with a mention of the old neighborhood. Recognition dawned as he smiled and extended a hand in friendship, if only for old times. We shook hands, showcasing our matured grips.

"Of course," he said. "I remember. How have you been? What are you doing?" He had just graduated from law school and was on the road to life. It had an enviable ring to it. We did the abbreviated little party dance, tagged with the door thing, underscored in its absurdity, considering I would never see most of these people again. From the corner of my eye, I noticed the sofa people still engrossed in their existential discussions. Almost through the crush at the door, I was overheated, and couldn't wait to leave and breathe fresh night air. Miles removed his coat, made his way into the party, and I left.

The hallway was dark. The hum of the elevator remained in my ear, well into the street. The subway was several blocks away and, at one in the morning, seemed even more distant. As I approached the desolate station, I became aware of the dull but persistent throb of a growing headache.

There weren't many passengers aboard the train when it finally arrived. I sat quietly as the long trip to my downtown Manhattan destination began. The passenger across from me was a homeless man, not especially menacing, but whose type had always stirred a kind of romantic wonder in me. Where was he from? What had brought him to this point in his life? Where was he going? Would he get there? Was the responsibility his? But instead of contemplating the man with romantic wonder, I found his quiet presence to cause in me growing anxiety and a distress. The more I tried to ignore it, the worse my headache became. The pulsating did not abate.

When I arrived home, I threw myself on the mercy of my bed. But the headache would not let me rest. I took aspirin and had a tall, icy cola, but the pain lingered. I went back to bed and tossed. The throbbing grew worse. When, I thought, did this start? What could have precipitated it? It was accompanied by a dreadful anxiety and a growing nausea. I felt extremely miserable. And it seemed to have been an uneventful, if not otherwise pleasant evening. Or was it? I thought it through. Seeing Manny Dunzler had annoyed me, was unpleasant, and raised some tension. But I had been aware of that. In truth, I didn't want to shake his hand; I would rather have taken a whack at his face. But although I contained my feeling, I hadn't really repressed it. I knew all along who he was, and I still didn't like him. I was going through the motions. Being civil; grown up.

The headache seemed to get worse. Like a migraine. It was almost as if it were trying to tell me something. Then I remembered. There was a sudden surge of awareness; a release of pressure. Zack Miles. I had shaken hands with him, too. It happened so soon on the heels of Dunzler; too quickly for me to have regained my psychological bearings.

For at least a couple of Halloweens, the celebrations had ceased to be fun and had given way to a kind of mini-terrorism. Venturing out and onto the streets of the neighborhood meant becoming prey to the older kids. The younger ones laid themselves open to a number of taunts. Zack Miles' favorite weapon was a long sock filled with ground chalk. He stalked the neighborhood and you never knew where he would appear. If he saw you, you were chalk dust. New jacket, suede jacket, wool jacket: Casper. Zack was my terror of Halloween.

It was a few days following a chalk drubbing that Zack extended a hand in friendship toward me. I was only about six years old but had my misgivings about any peace offering from him. I was, furthermore, well aware of the neighborhood's latest trick which could be perpetrated on an unsuspecting dupe by a more savvy wise guy.

"You're going to twist my arm," I said.

"No I won't," said Zack. "I promise."

I had just got a new cap gun, one of the few, new, metal guns made after the war.

"I know you'll twist my arm," I insisted.

"I swear I won't hurt you," said Zack. "If I do, you can hit me back." He extended his hand.

I shook Zack Miles' hand and he ducked beneath the two hands, turning about, twisting my arm. He no sooner had let it go than I swung wildly at his head…with my cap gun. Miles moved back but the pistol smacked his nose. It bled. He stood in shock. I said, "You said I could," but I had not foreseen the bloody consequence of my action. I regretted what I had done. And I think from that day I had been a pariah to Zack Miles.

The moment I recalled the event, the migraine vanished. I opened my window replacing the headache with fresh, night air.

Some years later, passing a Walden bookshop in a mall, I wondered what had become of us lords of life. Whimsically, I thought, I would check the passage in Wolfe's *Web and the Rock*. I remembered, on his twenty-first birthday, George Webber stood at the foot of the 42nd Street Library. He was "the Lord of Life." There was no such volume in the section marked "Literature." I asked the manager.

"Thomas Wolfe, of course. Follow me."

He took me all the way to the back of the store, to a section marked Social Studies. Social studies? Reaching down, he retrieved a copy of Tom Wolfe's *A Man in Full.*

"Wrong Wolfe," I said.

"Oh. Sorry. I don't know the other."

Obviously, I thought. So much for the lords of life. All of them.

The Story

Rossie, who had taken Gregory's handcuffs when they were both about five years old, was really his best friend. They would generally harass one another, like when Rossie would begin the "get ya last" game or when Gregory would take Rossie's hat and play "saloojie" with Mel, but for the most part there was a warm sense of buddyship between the two friends, and it extended toward, sometimes even centered around, Irv.

Now, Irv was Rossie's big brother. And everybody on the block who knew Irv thought he was a really great guy. Irv had had polio when he was just a kid and he limped. But he was huge. He told us once that he used to lift weights and do "Dynamic Tension" exercises when he was our age and that he was almost the strongest kid in the neighborhood. The only guy stronger than Irv was Jerry Ennis. And he was Irv's best friend. None of us ever saw Jerry Ennis or knew what he looked like, but we all knew, if you know what I mean. We all knew.

Most Saturdays, or sometimes in the evenings, you could see Irv taking his shirts to the Chinese laundry down on Broadway. There would be Rossie and Gregory standing in front of the apartment house; Rossie spitting a lot (Rossie had a compulsive spitting stage for about a year) and Gregory trying to do pull-ups from the last rung on the fire escape and there, as refreshing a sight for our bored eyes as ever, would come Irv, limping out of the house and down the steps with his shirts, smiling at us. He never ignored Rossie, but always seemed to have something to tell him about "upstairs." And when Gregory would wander over, that would start a conversation, usually about Jerry Ennis and the old days on the block. All the stories were about the same neighborhood, our neighborhood. But so much had changed. In fact, Irv was just about the only one left of the old days. All the others were gone. Not even Irv knew where.

Gregory was the first one to get a job at Harry's. Harry's was a candy store where, when you got to be an older kid on the block, you usually got a job helping out. You'd work nights from seven to nine, and in the afternoons, after school, from three to five. The best part of working at Harry's was jerking sodas behind the counter. Mostly that was at night. Rossie and the rest would come in and have Gregory mix some really wild sodas. Then we'd sit around and read the magazines. Harry always had pretty good magazines. Sometimes you got the feeling that Harry was annoyed with our being there, but usually he was too busy to follow through, what with one eye on the window and one ear on whatever violin music he had playing on his wooden portable radio perched on the shelf above the ice cream near the toys. So we stayed.

The worst part of working at Harry's was the afternoons. Because then you'd have to go down to the cellar with the dolly to carry up all the cases of Hoffman, Kirsh, Meyer, Pepsi, and Canada Dry that Harry thought he would be needing for that evening. You had to bring up syrup, too. Once Rossie dropped a whole bottle of Coke syrup after he had picked it up only to find one of those giant water bugs scurrying up the side of the jug. Rossie hated to pick up anything after that, and told Harry he wouldn't go down in that cellar unless the place was sprayed. And Harry eventually did get around to putting a certain white powder down there. But the bugs only seemed to get worse after that.

Rossie had first got the job at Harry's filling in for Gregory during the summer. Later, though, when summer vacation was over, he stayed on to work after school. Gregory wasn't allowed to work while he was in school.

Occasionally, after work, Gregory would cross the street to Rossie's house (it was really an apartment but they called it a house) and play Monopoly or Clue with him and Mel. Irv would sit in sometimes if he was home and tell about the old days in the street. Once he told us about how they were playing stickball downstairs and some guys from another neighborhood on the East Side wanted to take the game over—or else, they said, they would break it up. Irv, Jerry Ennis, and a few others took the whole lot of them on and sent them home crying. There might have been some older guys in our neighborhood right then, I thought, who could do the same thing, but I had never seen them fight. Chubby, Roger, Frenchy, Lucky, and Benny. They were all pretty tough.

Irv, of course, was downright strong. For instance, he could open any jar, no matter how tight the cover was stuck on. Once Gregory brought Irv a jar of guava marmalade from home that his father couldn't open. Gregory's father had said if he couldn't open it, no one could. And Gregory's father was pretty strong. Irv opened it, though. It took a little time and he had some trouble; he had to use hot water, but he opened it all right. Then we arm wrestled. What Irv used to do to show his strength sometimes, with a little coaxing, was Indian arm wrestle up to four of us; either one at a time, or all together. We never won. Irv's arm was like a rock.

On nice nights or before work, Rossie and Gregory liked to go to the park and work out on the bars. The ball field in the park had two sets of parallel bars and one set of horizontal bars. Mostly, guys would do dips on the parallel bars and chins and pull-ups on the horizontal bars. Rossie and Gregory were not the only ones who liked to hang around the bars. A kid named Billy Jones and a couple of his friends from way over on the east side of Broadway used to come to the park almost every day. Some of those guys were really great, too. They would do tricks like the "Giant," the "Penny-Drop," handstands, and even a few "muscle-ups," although none too gracefully and not even the "legal" way. Jones himself could never do a muscle-up, but he did a lot of swinging around and Gregory could do more pull-ups than he could. But whenever Jones and his bunch came to the ball field, Gregory wouldn't do too much. And Rossie would just stand around and spit.

One evening, when Gregory was walking Rossie home from Harry's, five guys sneaked up on them and one of them jumped Rossie. It was Billy Jones. Rossie had a bewildered look on his face and then he smiled.

20

"Whaddaya say, Billy?" he said. Billy still had an arm wrapped tight around Rossie's throat.

"Whaddaya say, Rossie?" Billy screamed. Then he got Rossie in a full nelson and one of the others punched Rossie in the stomach.

The last thing Gregory would ever do was run out on Rossie, but he didn't know what to do. Jones was too tough and the other guys just seemed to be standing around Jones and Rossie in a kind of circle. Then a couple of them joined in and started punching Rossie on the shoulder…like it was his birthday. Gregory stood and watched. But not for long, because the fat kid who had punched Rossie then punched Gregory in the stomach. It was a hard punch and surprisingly took Gregory's breath away, and for a long time, although he later told Rossie it didn't hurt that much. But he went down groaning and keeled over on his side. That seemed to satisfy them for the moment and all five of the Jones gang drifted away but said they would be waiting to get Rossie…later. So Rossie and Gregory went back to Harry's to call Irv.

Irv said he was on his way out to get the paper anyway and said they should wait for him. Rossie and Gregory were in the back reading the magazines over an egg-cream when Irv came in. He looked terrific. Calm as anything. He asked Rossie right away where Jones was. Rossie said he didn't know but that they were after him and Gregory.

"Come on," said Irv, "let's go." And they got up to go.

There was no sign of Billy Jones and his gang outside, and as we walked home together, Irv told a great story about how he and Jerry Ennis were being followed by two tough guys one evening on the very same street. He told us how Jerry turned around and grabbed one of the hoods in a headlock and started beating his face with this huge fist he had, and how when he finally let go, the kid just fell to the sidewalk and couldn't get up and the other guy took off. Irv said he didn't have to do a thing.

We didn't run into Billy Jones on the way home that night but we could imagine that tough kid lying on the sidewalk all those years ago, with his face smashed in, and we thought of Irv when he was younger, and the hood running away. And we thought of Irv and Jerry Ennis all the way back.

Lucky

I suppose the word best used to describe her then would be "lanky." It was a word I recall hearing more often then than now. Now, you might say "tall and thin." In the forties it was "lanky." Another word I recall hearing in reference to Mrs. Luckenbach was "divorcee." Now, that word is still in use, but it doesn't carry the same impact. It isn't as pejorative a word as it was in the 1940s. Then, it bore a stigma and was always whispered, although not too often, because Mrs. L was pretty much the only divorcee in the building...perhaps the only one on the block. Moreover, she wasn't seen all that frequently. But the really whispery thing about Mrs. L was the fact that she was, on more occasions than could be considered discreet, seen in the company of different men.

The first time I can remember seeing Mrs. L, she was arm-in-arm with a mustached man in a military trench coat and barracks cap. He was referred to as "the marine," and in fact was one...the first one I was ever aware of, if not the first I had ever seen. I recall him staggering his way home on Cabrini Boulevard on many afternoons and evenings and can recall overhearing disparaging comments by neighbors with regard to his sobriety. He was supposed to be Arthur and Bobby's father, or so we thought, but after he vanished and the years seemed to make more clear the marital status of Mrs. L, that idea was dismissed. Mrs. L was the mother of the boys. That was that. There was no father.

There was a grandmother, Mrs. L's mother. Pretty much it was she who took care of the boys. The old lady never left the apartment, but was frequently seen in her housedress and scuffs, shuffling her way between the apartment and the hallway incinerator. And often she could be heard yelling the boys' names into the street, her face and shoulders visible, leaning out of the third-floor window. Mrs. L apparently worked during the days and typically was seen arriving home in the evenings; unlike her mother, smartly dressed in a suit and heels, her hair always done up.

My first recollection of Bobby and Arthur was of the two of them, running across the street wearing sailor hats. It was soon after a ringworm scare and school inspection for the bug, complete with lamp lights and nurses. Beneath the boys' white hats, their heads were shaven.

They were both called "Lucky." The name seemed to fit each of them. Arthur was "Lucky." Bobby was "Lucky." Arthur was the younger but not by more than two years. Bobby was always the considerably taller. You might say he was… lanky. They bore no resemblance to one another, either physically or in their behavior. Bobby seemed quietly and confidently to enjoy the status of older brother. Arthur was the wilder and tougher, the more demonstrative and impetuous. But although Arthur was undeniably what kids referred to as tough, and maybe even the toughest on the block, he was not, as many a "tough" kid was, psychotic, volatile, or nasty. He was approachable. And contrary to utilizing his "tough" status to bully, Arthur was often prevailed upon by younger, smaller, or weaker kids to protect, defend, or help them out of a jam with less-understanding denizens of the neighborhood. He was a good arbitrator, mostly because he could negotiate from a position of strength. And he never exacted anything for the service.

Bobby sometimes played stickball with the older kids on the block, but was less of a presence than was his brother. He kept to himself. Shortly after the Korean War broke out, I seem to recall Bobby jauntily arriving in the neighborhood one afternoon in a sailor suit. I say "seem to recall" because I can't figure how he had got hold of the uniform so fast, and perhaps over the years, I had only imagined him as a fully-outfitted sailor, somewhat prematurely. In any case, he was back in civilian clothes some days later. Word was he was turned down, and reclassified 4-F because of a punctured eardrum. The rejection became known from the neighborhood buzz, and the feeling was that for Bobby, pride had turned to shame. It had, at least for him, become disappointment.

Arthur, meanwhile, was becoming sinewy, although not nearly reaching the height of his older brother, and developing his lean, muscular frame by some mysterious process, which, when I queried him about it, he did confide, could be attributed to strenuous weightlifting at home... barbells! It was the first I had ever heard of this process. Shortly thereafter, from spring through the fall, Arthur rarely wore anything but T-shirts with sleeves rolled up to the shoulders, unfiltered package of cigarettes tucked securely in the folds. And soon after that, he became the first on the block to sport a tattoo on his deltoid. It was a red heart with an arrow piercing it. Beneath it, it said "Mother." I remember many brief evening conversations, with Arthur perched on the fender of a parked car, during which he waxed knowledgeable on any one of a number of subjects. Arthur had the wisdom of a kid who was three or four years older than you were. He knew about weightlifting, women, sharp dressing, and, it seemed, the adventuring ways of the world. Later that year, Arthur enlisted, impressively, in the U.S. Air Force. The feeling was that Bobby felt badly.

Arthur was killed shortly thereafter while stationed out west. The story had it as being a car accident somewhere on the coast. For most of us word of what had happened carried a most unreal quality and did not convey the kind of devastating, tragic impact it should have. It had the undertone of another wild event; another bit of the kind of rash mischief that characterized much of what Arthur did. How he lived. And for some time, the expectation was that someday, somehow, Arthur would be coming back.

Less and less was seen of Bobby, and it seemed the days of carefree stickball and frivolous hanging around outside, in romp and high jinks, had passed. With Arthur's vanishing from the ranks, something of the cavalier was gone from the block. When I did see Bobby, he never smiled, he never laughed. He seemed sullen. Bitter. And always to himself, dissuading any casual conversation.

We moved to the apartment above the Luckenbachs. I was attending high school and playing piano. And just about everyone within earshot knew. One day a strange thumping sound, a persistent bass vibration, began to emanate from the floorboards. It was not long afterwards that Bobby Luckenbach one afternoon rang my doorbell.

It was a warm spring afternoon and the promise of the school term's end; an exciting summer, romance and all the indefinable options open to youth, softened and tantalized the air. It was the kind of air so gentle and undisturbing, its benevolence almost went unnoticed, certainly unappreciated. But it was there. And it seemed to me, at least in subsequent years, to have colored and set the tone for everything that happened that entire afternoon.

It was the first time I had ever seen Bobby Luckenbach standing at my door. Up front and person-to-person, so to speak. An older kid. I was totally puzzled as to what he might have wanted. It crossed my mind my playing might have gone too far and his visit was by way of a complaint. Bobby said he knew I played the piano and that I was attending a music high school and he wanted to show me something. He said he would appreciate my opinion. Really, he had wanted to share something with me. Obviously, there was no one else.

We went downstairs and for the first time, I ventured through the Luckenbach door. The old lady was there, in her housedress, shuffling about. Bobby took me through the long hallway into his room at the back of the apartment. With an indescribable pride, he showed me his high-fidelity set up: the speakers, the amps, the turntable, the receiver. And then with great delicacy, he lovingly removed several records from a neat array of albums carefully organized on new, dust-free shelves. The albums were: Frank Sinatra with the Nelson Riddle Orchestra, and a guy I had never heard of, Stan Kenton. The room filled with a vibrating "Artistry in Rhythm" and "Opus in Pastels," "Laura" and "Intermission Riff." I now understood where the thumping bass in the floorboards came from and heard a combination of sounds I had never heard before called "23 Degrees North 82 Degrees West"; synchronized trombones that haunted me for years until I finally learned what the title meant and located the recording. (It turned out to be the coordinates of Havana, Cuba.) And then Bobby played Sinatra's "I've Got You Under My Skin," snapping his fingers to the Nelson Riddle arrangement. I had never seen him smile so broadly and so much. I had never seen him as happy. Since then, Sinatra/Riddle and Stan Kenton have always been connected for me, and spring days have always borne the strains and echoes of those tunes; the music those men made.

I had completed my first year at Hunter College when Bobby asked me down to hear some new Kenton sides he had just bought. He told me he had gotten a job at a neighborhood record store. And soon, he said, he would be going for his "G.E.D." He smiled a wide grin, revealing a row of crooked, somewhat poorly aligned, concave top teeth.

The last time I saw Bobby Lucky he was busy with customers in the mom-and-pop record shop on 181st Street between Broadway and Fort Washington Avenue. He was laughing, in motion, totally involved.

The Port of New York Authority razed our apartment building shortly thereafter. All the 20 Cabrini tenants had to relocate and I never saw Bobby after that, although on many spring afternoons, I wondered where Bobby Lucky and his mother had flown to and whether Bobby was still hearing the sounds he had loved. He didn't seem to be listed anywhere, not under any of the spellings I tried for his name. It was, after all, a tricky name. Luckenback? Luchenbach? Luckenbach? Or was it Luckenbacher? It wasn't Lucky.

It was on a balmy June day more than forty years later that I ventured into the New York Public Library on 42nd Street to see if I could get the proper spelling of Bobby's last name from an old listing in a 1949 reverse telephone directory. And what was his mother's name, anyway? Perhaps, I thought, his number might still be listed under her name. I had always thought it was Mary…or Marion.

Finding the proper room on the second floor, Local History, I accessed the telephone book on a reel of microfiche. And there it was: 20 Cabrini Boulevard with a listing of nearly all the tenants I had remembered; many of them quite gone and many quite forgotten. But something was wrong because Lucky wasn't there. Neither was Luchenback, Luckenbach, or any other similar spelling. It took me a moment and then I realized, of course! They didn't have a telephone yet! I tried a 1950 book. My finger caressed the screen, moving down the list of long-lost, familiar, and now regained names. There they all were, as they had been. And there was Lucky's. I might not find him now, after all these years, but I had found his name. Luckenbach. And the first name, unexpected. It was Bobby's and Arthur's mother. Her name, strange and uncommon. Kind of classy sounding. A lovely name: Marlan. It didn't seem to fit her. But the more I looked at it, the more I looked back, the more I guess it did. The more it fit. Anyway, there it was. Marlan. Marlan Luckenbach. There it was.

Gary Alexander Azerier

The Scooter

There was no Dick and Jane. The first literary hero whose exploits I joyfully anticipated reading was Tom…of Tom and Nancy. These were the two protagonists (although they did not seem to suffer in the least) who ushered us all, in Mrs. Callanan's 1A, into the wonderful world of pages. They passed us the keys, showed us how to lift the inky words to the light, revealing the color; the stories and the friends the words carried. Tom and Nancy taught us how distracting, how exciting and compelling paper pages could be. And the words were the bridges between thought and imagination. But sometimes the lessons got lost in confusion, oddly brought about.

There was the steady flow of tears each day for a while from Nancy Solomon, one of the five-year-olds in our class. I felt complete incomprehension. But her crying was because her name, her private and personal name was carried by Nancy, our heroine, and read aloud by all. Nancy, the student, bitterly complained to her friend Nicole that too much attention was now focused upon her, thanks to the common name. She was no longer sheathed in tolerable anonymity. She now shared attention with the Nancy of fiction, which she did not sport comfortably. Perhaps either or both of them were teased, made fun of, pointed to or singled out, and a slight to one was a slight to the other. And maybe Nancy felt her simple life could not compare to our heroine's exploits; the romance, the adventure. I remember Nicole placing a consoling hand on Nancy's convulsing shoulder, saying, "I know. I know how you feel; it used to happen to me." I wondered about that. Such sagacity. Such worldliness.

I, on the other hand, wholly identified with Tom. What Tom did, I wanted to do. Tom was my hero. His deeds stood out sharply. They were well-defined. What he did was right; the thing to do. And, it was fun.

The most exciting thing I can recall about Tom was his skates. He had a pair of roller skates. It was my favorite page; the page on which Tom put on his skates. There was an illustration of our hero, rosy-cheeked and pink-faced, seated on a stoop, putting on his skates. It was always the first page I turned to when Mrs. Callanan said: "Take out your readers." The following page had Tom skating. There wasn't much more to the episode than that, but it was enough. It reaffirmed my identity. It reinforced my interest. It reasserted my goal for the end of the day. Like Tom, when school was out, I would go home, put on my roller skates, and like Tom, my friend and hero, I too would skate.

Fortunately, I had the skates. At my grandmother's apartment in the Bronx, only a couple of trolley car rides away from Washington Heights, not counting the bus that took us through Crotona Park, to Bryant Avenue, there was one magical spot for me. It was the corner of a hallway closet where my grandmother kept a pair of Everlast boxing gloves and a pair of skates.

On the Saturdays my mother and I visited, it defined how I spent the afternoon. First stop: The closet! They were still there! I put on the skates and the boxing gloves and exhausted the next few hours skating around the apartment's wood floors, wearing the oversized boxing gloves.

One day, when the war was over and my uncles came home, the skates became mine! They were steel, and for the duration of the war and a time afterward, they could not be found for sale anywhere. Unlike the Rollerblades of the future, these marvels had no attached shoe or boot; they clamped to the sole of your shoe, strapped around your ankle, and got fastened with your skate key, a wrench-like tool made to fit around a small iron rod beneath the skate. This could be rotated, which in turn tightened (or loosened) the front clamps and sent you on your way, skate key hanging around your neck on a piece of string, the entire affair soon to be lost. "Could I borrow your skate key?"

On the concrete sidewalks, roller skates hardly characterized stealth. The clatter was unmistakable and disturbing, even to the skater, and often forced him or her off the sidewalk into a smoother, quieter, tarred gutter, however parent-frowned-upon because of oncoming traffic. "Don't skate in the street!"

So it was, expedited by the difficulties and dangers inherent in roller skating, that with little objection or resistance, and minimal regret after a year or so, the skates followed the path of natural skate evolution. And as the egg becomes the chick, as the caterpillar becomes the butterfly, the skate became…the scooter.

Mostly during the autumn, sometimes with the approach of spring, homemade scooters began to appear. They tore down hills and ripped around corners, the front rider's foot frantically pumping at the street, his hands grasping the orange crate top. Sometimes the coachman squatted down behind the box, navigating through slats. Sometimes the chauffeur rode two, as a surprise passenger would appear after a harrowing ride, grasping knees, keeping balance, and ducking low, until the last moment. This tactic was useful in war games and smuggling spies into enemy camps.

All you needed was a crate, a two-by-four slat, some nails, and a pair of skates. Actually, one skate was enough, since it came apart. The front got nailed to one end of the two-by-four's underside, the rear wheels fastened to the opposite end.

I never got the large orange crate. My box was smaller. It was the only crate the fruit store man had left. It had held peaches. But it made my contraption look different. Across the top were handlebars (which I never held, holding instead to the box itself), and to make it unique, I inserted a shelf about four inches from the top for magazines; a kind of glove compartment. It could also hold cupcakes and a snack. I even hung a little cloth over the shelf. A kind of curtain. We didn't own a car, but I was determined to remedy that. This was my vehicle.

Perhaps the most unusual feature of this contraption was that my mother allowed it into the apartment. Most of the kids on the block kept theirs in the cellar. But not mine. Not my cream puff. My mother might have drawn the line had I used an orange crate. But the peach box made the cut.

On chilly fall days I recall taking the thing down in the elevator, its shelf fully stocked with magazines, cookies, and gloves. For the most part, I only sat around our corner on 178th Street and read the magazines, my trusty steed at my side. I never even ventured down the block.

When differences arose at home, and feelings were chafed, I knew I could easily pack the scooter and hop aboard the next day, and before you knew it be well on my way to…who could say? Maybe as far as Oklahoma! Texas! Even though I had hardly ever gotten as far as two blocks. But one day, if they pushed far enough, I would just head south.

I once owned an old Oldsmobile. It was my first car. It was exciting. At the end of the first week I had it, I drove from North Carolina to New York. But it could never have taken me as far as that scooter.

In the days of the scooter, just for some perspective, there were three major auto makers in the U.S.: Ford, GM, and Chrysler. Top of the line was Lincoln, Cadillac, and Chrysler. The more economical cars included the Chevy, Ford, and Plymouth. In between were Dodge, Desoto, Pontiac, Oldsmobile, and Buick. There was also a smattering of oddball cars: Hudson, Nash, Studebaker, Packard, Kaiser-Fraser. But not so many you couldn't keep track.

There have been countless automobiles since; hundreds. But never, anywhere, has there ever been a machine that rode so smooth, that was as powerful, that looked so neat, and that could take you as far as that 1947 scooter. They just don't build them like that anymore. But there is another factor which should be noted.

There was this tiny, little four-year-old I saw just the other day. She couldn't have stood more than two and a half feet off the ground. She was riding, ever so slowly, a shiny, sleek, store-bought, state-of-the-art scooter. She was battened down with a helmet that must have weighed more than she did. The thing had more belts, straps, and eyelets than you could fasten in a month and most likely cost more than the scooter. It was a manufacturer's coup.

Just looking at it, I knew the little girl's scooter couldn't have gone to Oklahoma. It didn't have the power, it didn't have a secret, private compartment, and with that helmet over her eyes, you couldn't even see the fun in front of you. It was no peach crate. They just don't make them like that anymore.

SUMMER

Palisades Park

Summer. Heat. Periodic emptiness and quiet afternoons. Sometimes going "downstairs" and stepping outside onto Cabrini Boulevard was like walking into the dry heat of the much-spoken-of oven. Together with the stillness and silence of the one-way, nearly dead end street, (you could only turn east on 178th Street) there were few better comparisons. The noises, the people, the activity on hot July and August days seemed to be sucked away along with any semblance of comfortable temperatures or amenable air. On some late mornings and early afternoons the vacant sidewalks of the block between 177th and 178th streets brought the Devil's Anvil, or Frying Pan, or any number of implements, to mind. And when no friends were out, there were few diversions from the discomfort; few amusements. It was too hot to play. No breezes blew.

There were, however, occasional distractions. On long, oppressively hot weekends during those days, when air conditioning was not a commonplace feature in

Washington Heights apartments, my father—who was not a moviegoer—would offer to treat my mother and me to "an air-conditioned movie." It did not matter what was playing. And the gleeful surprise of this was sustained, sometimes over an entire three-day holiday weekend, when we saw not one or two, but three days of films. In the forties and fifties, with double features, this was no less than six films, not to mention newsreels and selected short subjects. Sometimes it was better than going away. It killed entire afternoons; certainly it was cheaper. But it simply occurred when my father got on a kick; that is, found something that worked.

In those pre-air-conditioned apartment days, when drives out of the city were not options because we did not own a car, some choices that required little travel, expense, or arrangements still remained as desperate attempts to escape the heat. One of these was an afternoon on the rooftop in hopes of catching a zephyr; another was a picnic along the Henry Hudson Parkway, for which my father prepared a small cooler of his famous Tom Collins. I am confident he carried the gin separately but the elixir in the jug, no more than ice cubes and Canada Dry Tom Collins Mix, tasted special, forever to be associated with cool, grassy picnics; the glory of the Hudson to the west, the great bridge to the north.

There were days when a walk over the entire span of the George Washington beckoned. The heat had to be a bit more moderate, for the walk was considerable, although there were the promises of breezes, watery vistas, and the wonderful assurances of a little refreshment stand at the end of the bridge in Fort Lee, New Jersey. It was here you could get Coca-Cola in the small green glass bottle, and the unique footlong hot dog, boiled in oil; the reward of a summer day, the rainbow at the end of the bridge.

But looking west from the span of the great bridge revealed wonders greater than the little refreshment stand. From the north side of the bridge you could see the bright neon blue and red of Bill Miller's Riviera; an oasis of adult festivity and gaiety, a nightclub, whose home was in the Garden State of New Jersey, embraced by space and a view of the river, not the grim, subway-accessible crowdedness of downtown New York City. This place was more appealing, romantic, and magical. It was fresher, but as yet, a mystery. Riviera!

Looking to the southwest, as we often could on clear days in our neighborhood, there was the wonderful visual whisper of fun, the suggestion of joy across the Hudson, as the top of the great cyclone teased our eye and imagination with Palisades Amusement Park. It was something far away, myth. Yet you could almost touch it as hopes brought it within reach.

Sometime just before the close of school, with the approach of summer, certain discount tickets for Palisades Park materialized in the neighborhood. They were printed to look like real tickets and bore the illusion of Free Ticket to Palisades Amusement Park. Of course, the tickets were themselves given away as free, but only provided a small discount with the general admission. And perhaps an additional discount was given on certain rides or attractions. I was very impressed with these attractive-looking tickets and began to collect them until I had amassed what I thought to be a fortune in discounts. It took awhile before I realized the tickets didn't amount to much, and gave up the dream of somehow cashing in at the gate. But just the look of the Palisades logo and the graphics…the word "amusement"…; the holding of tickets to Palisades….

One summer day, somehow I prevailed. My father, not especially a fan of amusement parks, took my mother and me to New Jersey and Palisades Amusement Park.

It was the kind of day you might expect at an amusement park. Rides, cotton candy, and games of skill and chance. In retrospect, it seems sad trying to extract fun, joy, and excitement out of a mini-trip in or on a machine that spins or lifts, jolts you for a few minutes. But that's what it was; that, and the excitement of waiting to see what was next.

What fascinated me most that day was what seemed like an inordinate number of kids toting about giant toys, stuffed pandas and other colorful kewpies. My father must have noticed my coveting stares and gravitated to a game of chance. It was a wheel of fortune type device with matching numbers printed on the counter on which you placed your bet. Bets were a dime. Nickels were more the thing in those days. Dimes indicated a bit of excess cost. I didn't anticipate a second wager after he had lost the first but my father tried again. We lost again. I am sure we all had a sense of the old carnie rip-off but apparently determined to win the giant panda, my father bet again and again, graduating to wager several dimes on each spin…and then several dimes on each of several numbers.

It couldn't have been that much money, but it sure seemed like it. My father changed dollar bills, and bet and bet again. I had heard him tell stories of how he and his father had visited a casino in Russia when he was a boy and how his father, who had died a very young man, had won. How close they had become that night; how they were winners. But no matter how many thin Mercury dimes my father placed on the counter, no matter on what numbers, he could not win. I watched the man in the booth sweep the dimes off the painted numbers into a trough and fistful them into his apron pockets. My father changed more dollar bills into dimes and put his money on the table with great purpose and little indecision; as if he had an inside tip as to how the wheel would go. I wondered at how many times anyone could lose consecutively without one win. That was all he wanted. It no longer had any connection to the giant panda. But we were on either the right or the left side of the winning number, or far from it. We never won.

When we left Palisades Amusement Park that afternoon, I felt blue, certainly compared with what you might expect after an afternoon at an amusement park. But it was I who had brought my father to Palisades. He had spent countless dimes, amounting to dollars he could ill afford, because of me.

What had me feeling saddest of all was not our failure to win anything, but knowing the real reason my father wanted to win. He wanted to be a winner in the eyes of his son. But it was my knowledge that he felt he had failed in that. My father thought he was a loser. The fact is though, he really wasn't.

Gun Hill Road

The seasons we enjoyed and even savored in Washington Heights were marked, not especially by sunshine or snow, falling leaves or chill. Should you have happened on them as they were in progress, these seasons were marked by something more tangible, something you could carry or tuck in a pocket, something you could take home with you: knick-knacks, trinkets, toys. When pockets of jackets and trousers were soaked by leaky (there was no way to get around it) water pistols, more familiarly called water guns, spring was close by. Bubble gum cards and cereal premiums typically made their arrival concurrent with the start of the school term; autumn and spring brought along the yo-yo and the pea-shooter, as well as roller skates and bikes; winter was identified by less portable hockey sticks and Flexible Flyers; and summer…more than anything else, more than bats and gloves, more than soda and ice pops in the street, the promise of summer, the explosive joy of summer freedom and the frivolity of the months ahead was heralded by the sudden appearance, the incomparable, exotic and mysterious appearance of…the firecracker.

Predictably, the plaything of the season would make its debut in school: in the school yard, in the hallway, or—much to the consternation of the teachers—in the classroom. The object was generally in motion, being passed from one kid to another, traveling from aisle to aisle, for examination, admiration or trade, or, less gracefully but more conspicuously, sailing through the air, across desks, over heads, and sometimes inadvertently finding its way to the dreaded front of the room. Generally before that happened, however, and before the thing was confiscated, it had already been introduced to all, and had become quite familiar, enjoying the quickly attained status as a must-have, and soon to be much sought after knick-knack of desire.

Very often, acquiring the object was no simple matter. Its origin was shrouded in mystery and sometimes secrecy, the whereabouts of its point of purchase or appropriation described so vaguely or inarticulately that for the early owners of the object, exclusivity was insured. But not for long. Frequently, the matter of acquisition was resolved by the name and location of a simple novelty shop or candy store. Not always.

In the case of a water gun of a specific design or yo-yo of a particular brand (Duncan and Cheerio were the only ones that carried any status for us), or magazine of questionable content, it was only a matter of time before the store, usually nearby the school, was sold out of the item, and nearly everyone owned the coveted puzzle, trick, comic, or toy. On occasion, however, something made an appearance in our midst that was so secret, was cloaked in such tight-lipped security and mystery and was handled by such shadowy distributors as to make its ready availability to the more pedestrian among us, less than possible and only a dream. Such was the aura about the firecracker.

The arrival of the firecracker was usually preceded by a vendor selling sparklers from a box on a street corner. Soon afterwards, pops and crackles could be heard throughout the neighborhood and occasionally, though rarely inside school (far too risky) one would catch a glimpse of an unopened, gaily decorated, paper package in the possession of some lucky kid who enjoyed sudden status, instant prestige. And yet, the source, the wellspring of these little packages was nowhere to be found. In the school yard or on the streets, packages or loose firecrackers simply seemed to materialize and then vanish in puffs of smoke. And sometimes, in the park, behind a bench, half-buried in dirt, one would unearth a shredded wrapper. But scrutinize it as one might, there were few clues as to its origin.

A little while into the season of the firecracker, a station wagon or a van would make an appearance on one of the quiet side streets of the neighborhood. At times, there was no vehicle, but an older teen on foot or even a young man with a shady look, toting a small satchel, would draw a crowd of kids, and while we bystanders stretched our necks to see what was behind the van's back seat, or in the bag, for a dime or fifteen cents a package, the seller would distribute his wares to the more affluent among us. The more expensive fireworks, apparently not slated for any of us, if for no reason other than price, were only rarely espied. And, if you were not buying, it was not considered acceptable to touch, ask about, or even get a better glimpse of the merchandise. The only place those more exotic wares were going was somewhere into our imaginations, where they would bed down and acquire strange forms for years.

The forms we did become somewhat familiar with were called Ladyfingers, Two Inchers, Ash Cans, Cherry Bombs, Rockets, and Torpedoes. And, not particularly enamored by the curt treatment received from our brusque neighborhood purveyor of these little explosives, we sought possible additional outlets. There did not seem to be any.

I walked from block to block, candy store to candy store, especially in neighborhoods more remote than my own, inquiring whether the owner sold "firecrackers." All of them answered "no," although there were some I suspected of hiding the truth as well as the firecrackers. I was convinced that hordes of them lay hidden beneath the counter or secreted away in a back room, awaiting a more familiar customer, privy to some password, or one who could offer a tactful bribe. Attracting particular suspicion in my eyes were candy store owners who appeared to be recent arrivals to this country or the neighborhood. It seemed logical to me they had some pipeline to, some firecracker contact in, a distant but accessible foreign country. What kept me driven and obsessed with these notions was that firecrackers were understood to be, known by all to be (and yet obtainable by some), illegal.

To come by fifteen cents of disposable money in those days was almost as difficult as procuring a package of firecrackers. But by zealous collecting of two-cent deposit bottles and scouring the curbsides for the infrequent coin, and the judicious dispensing of these funds, it was possible to gain select admission into the inner sanctum.

Billy Simon was a loner. He was a year or so older than I, seemed to skirt propriety at times, although not flagrantly, and I had heard he owned, and for not too steep a price would sell, firecrackers. It was true. And one afternoon I found him and showed him my fifteen cents. He accommodatingly led me through the alley between 177th and 176th streets, at Pinehurst Avenue, knelt before a small drain, and lifted the six- or seven-inch square cover. Beneath it were several packages of Devil Brand firecrackers. My eyes wide, I thought, had I only known this was where he kept them! But of course, by then, it was too late. Simon would be using a new hiding place.

As it happened, during these early days of summer, there was some kind of gypsy moth mini-infestation of the trees, and the little worms were scattered about on the sidewalks beneath. My friend Noah and I gathered up some of these tiny things, and unable to control my enthusiasm or utilize any functioning part of my brain to think my plot through, I collected the worms, stuffed them into a pill bottle, and decided what a clever idea it might be if we were to add a firecracker into the package and blow them all to kingdom come. It eluded me that the container was glass and might not be equal to containing the blast. I did not foresee little shards of glass being sprayed about. But that, of course, was what happened.

A tiny tyke was passing with a slightly older girl when the blast went off. She began to cry as I noticed a trickle of blood coming from her tiny knee. Stunned, I could not comprehend how the cut and the bleeding could have simply appeared. I went to check the fate of the worms and my pill bottle. There was no bottle.

to depart, for a few weeks at an upstate camp, on
ng day. And as I sat in my living room sharing a
...day afternoon lunch with my parents, I fervently hoped
to make it through the day, and onto tomorrow's camp bus,
without any repercussions owing to the incident which had
just occurred. But I knew I was soon to be nailed by the kind
of trouble which was in hot pursuit.

We kept the front door open to allow circulation of air
from the hallway, but it was not only the breeze which blew
into our apartment. To my horror, standing before our door
with his little girl and her babysitter was the child's stocky,
golf-shirt-clad father. He peered into our living room as the
babysitter pointed at me. "That's him," she said.

It was rare that I found myself in this kind of accusatory
trouble. It was anathema to my father, a quiet and a just
man, and he tensed, sinking into an apparent state of shock
at the man's glowering and clenched expression. Confused
and taken by surprise, he paled.

My father, a law school graduate, was well aware, even
in those days, of the possible consequences of damages
and a lawsuit. But somehow, due to a combination of his
diplomacy and the relatively insignificant nature of the little
girl's cut, the initially irate man was pacified by whatever
words or promises my assuaging father had lulled him with.
Then he left with his little troupe and we never saw him again.
My next day's bus escape to camp took place, but, tongue
lashed and reprimanded, remaining firecrackers confiscated,
warned, admonished and lectured, the departure was not a
smooth one. The lingering feeling, laden with guilt, was that
I had lost innocence in the eyes of my parents. Evidently,
though, I did not turn out to be quite the malevolent ogre in

the eyes of the tiny girl's father that he may have expected; that I was made out to be by the little girl's babysitter.

Two-thirds of the summer having passed, I returned from camp and I supposed all, at least most, had been forgiven. The firecrackers stayed confiscated and hidden somewhere in my father's possession. I was not especially anxious to resume my mischievous ways, but the old fascinations lingered. And Noah had not been stung by the finger pointing, accusing incident I had suffered which shamed and scared me into reforming my ways.

Noah and a friend of ours, Jon Mayer, had not only managed to discover, definitively, the origin of the firecrackers, but had determined to locate and purchase them.

Noah, who has since gone on to hold a doctorate in biology, and who at one point decided to study medicine in Paris when he was in his forties, was well-known in our circle, if not the entire neighborhood, as an extremely bright, precocious, and mischievous character. He had a kind of local notoriety. And once an amusing challenge had been posed, no matter the prohibition, Noah was not to be deterred or dissuaded in his pursuit. Jon, who went on to become a consummate jazz piano player and perhaps one of the most innovative in the United States from his base in California, was perhaps more cautious in his approach to the lure than Noah, but was equally daring and not one to heed bans, taboos, or proscriptions. The sign "off limits" did not apply to either of them, and the two made a formidable team, equal to the task of venturing forth on their excursion into the Bronx. They thought.

Jon and Noah, with the vacancy of summer in which to thrash around, honed in on what I had thought to be a rumor. Oddly enough, it turned out to be true. Firecrackers, indeed stores of fireworks of all kinds, could be found—and purchased—at a place in the Bronx called, ironically, Gun Hill Road.

So the duo, at twelve years of age, found the Lexington Avenue subway, no mean feat from the west side, and made their way to the much-touted Gun Hill Road, a considerable distance and a borough away from Washington Heights. Once there, it was Noah who led Jon to someone's back yard, where the merchandise was spread out in all its wonder and abundance. And with all of a few dollars to spend (although subway fares were only a dime) they bought their stash. Noah, in his anticipation, foresight, and optimism had brought a small bag with him in which to pack the loot. Jon, whose ill preparation was brought about by doubts and misgivings, had only wide pockets in his jeans.

There before them were the Rockets, Roman Candles, Fountains, and Firecrackers they had dreamed of; the objects of all desire. There, in bare seductive availability, were all the colors, the mysteries, the promise. No one would have believed it. Could they keep it quiet? In part, that was why Noah had taken Jon. Noah had been there earlier, by himself, with no one to share it with. He had scouted it out before, alone. Now the pleasures were doubled for the two of them. They picked and chose and spent everything they had.

Gun Hill Road was neither the most hospitable nor the safest place for a couple of twelve-year-olds alone; strangers with a satchel and bulging pocketsfull of firecrackers. It was not long before Jon and Noah realized they were being followed. Some older kids, the arch enemies of younger kids, had either seen them making the buy or realized what they were carrying. Jon and Noah knew, too late, they should have waited before examining what they had just bought, before inviting the attentions of the street's untoward elements. They hurried to the elevated train station.

The train was just arriving on the platform, with the ruffians no longer slowly trailing behind, but already having broken into a run, as Jon and Noah jumped aboard. The group of three or four pursuers stood lurking at the back of the subway car and began to inch closer to the two boys. It was then that Jon came up with his clever scheme. He whispered to Noah that at the next stop, they would stall for some moments, pretending not to be ready to get off, then, at the very last second, they would make a mad dash and leap off the train. They did. But the doors stayed open too long and the Gun Hill toughs got off as well. There they were, at a desolate and strange station in the Bronx, approached and slowly surrounded by the bullies who had just materialized into Jon's carefully-thought-out escape plan. It seemed, Wile E. Coyote-like, to fall under the heading of: "Whoops!"

Noah, bearer of the bag, was relieved of his tote and its contents. Jon was taken for a bystander, and returned to the Heights with Noah, along with his stash of half a dozen or so packages, pretty much intact. They sold each for the nickel or dime per package profit, and may have come away, as nearly everything seems to render us, a bit the wiser.

No fewer than forty years later, when I should long have forgotten such adventures and might also have dispensed with such lingering fascinations, for the first time, I was to drive the Northeast Corridor along Route 95 to Florida, about to embark on the great automobile excursion I had been denied in my youth because we had not then owned a car. Now, my deprivation was about to be redeemed. Somehow, I was intent on compensating myself for all those years of wanting.

Along the way, as the weather seemed to become balmier, I was delighted by the interminable South of the Border signs through North Carolina. But it was nothing compared to the bold billboards advertising the fireworks to be had in the many outlets of what the signs throughout South Carolina proclaimed as the "Fireworks Capital of the World!"

I prevailed on my wife to stop and look into one of these emporiums. She was amicable to consent and delay the journey for a few moments, but was not all that impressed. I, on the other hand, was stunned, staggered, and awed. I had not been on the Noah/Jon adventure that long-ago summer afternoon, nor had I ever seen a display of fireworks in abundance…certainly within reach. The only thing I had ever seen on Gun Hill Road was Montefiore Hospital.

The fireworks place was astonishing. It was a supermarket of explosives ranging in price from pennies to many dollars. The items were available by the piece, package, box, or carton. There were the expected Rockets and Roman Candles, but also more imaginative pieces: Chinese Fountains, Gushing Fountains, Flower Gardens, Hanging Gardens, Whistling Fountains, Sparkling Whistles. There were Devils, Dragons, Black Cats, Blue Demons, White Angels, Green Geysers. I bought nearly one of each kind. I was twelve years old again.

When I got back home, after driving through states like Virginia, and the city of New York, where such pyrotechnics are illegal, I unpacked my bounty and when I was alone, spread the nicely packaged pieces out before me. There they were, almost as they might have been then, in the forties, in the shady purveyor's van; in the back room of the candy store; in the strange and bottomless satchel of the entrepreneur teenage kid; on Gun Hill Road. And it was just about all there: Exploding Hens and Roosters, Fountains, Sparkling Tanks, Cones and Cylinders, Desert Camels, and Oriental Bloomers. I certainly had an assortment and a sampling of everything I had ever wanted or imagined. There was nothing left to find. It was a veritable fire hazard.

I looked at the colorful display on the floor. Lovely. But not quite what Noah and Jon had sought...and found. They would remember forever what they had pursued, obtained, and lost. Or had they really lost it? I, however, was now faced with the task of getting rid of this stuff. I looked at my satchel next to the strange little heaps of contraband. Moments ago it had held much. It had been so full. Now, a bit squashed, it was empty.

Narrowsburg

For two memorable summers, in 1949 and 1950, my parents rented a room at a large upstate New York farm so we could escape the oppressive city heat of July and August. So, come June 30, my mother and I, (my father was working), boarded a train, pulled away from Washington Heights, and were off to spend eight bucolic weeks in Narrowsburg, New York.

Years later, after having purchased a vacation home in the Pocono Mountains of Pennsylvania, I saw a road sign that said "Narrowsburg." Following the word was a designated route number. I filed the sighting away, excited by hopes of finding the old farm, and nebulous intentions to follow the sign in days to come.

It did take awhile to seriously embark on the journey, and finding the farm wasn't easy. It wasn't there anymore. The land had been cleared of the farmhouse and adjacent structures, now buried in the past for good. Furthermore, it had taken several tries just to have gotten that far.

I had found the town, Narrowsburg: a restaurant, barber shop, novelty and gift store, post office, railroad depot. Seeing it almost as it had been elicited momentary rejuvenation and a great joy. There was a nice overlook commanding a scenic view of parkland and water, which I didn't remember. But standing before the train depot brought back that hot summer afternoon in 1950.

My mother and I had disembarked and taken our bags to stand before the train depot, in the street, overdressed, waiting for Old Man Schwartz to arrive in his black pickup truck to take us down the back roads to the farm.

Peculiarly, as I thought back to that day and the scene appeared vividly to me, I was overtaken by an all-encompassing depression. It was not a simple wistfulness. I was smitten with a deep gloom. My impression was that something had happened on that spot, that very afternoon. I did not know what. As I allowed myself to drift back to 1950, I saw myself, the eleven–year-old, holding a paper pocket calendar hidden behind an arithmetic text book.

I had begun counting and crossing off days as early as the end of April, the little card calendar, one of my most cherished pocket treasures, produced at every available opportunity. High point of the afternoon was the moment reserved for obliterating another passed school day. It was also my habit to keep at least four or five days behind so I could occasionally annihilate more than one or even two days at a time. And by the end of May, the ritual was embraced in earnest.

The yo-yo I had been saving for and with which I envisioned myself spending endless hours in amusement and practice was to be a bright green Duncan with black stripe. I had already purchased glassine bags of spare strings. I imagined waiting for my friends on the farmhouse porch, filling any dull moments with the Duncan. It would be a tension-free summer of relaxation and play. I had had enough of tests, homework, schools, and teachers.

The train ride was wonderful. It was part of what I had been looking forward to: the dining car breakfast of pancakes, the linen napkins and heavy silvery urns, the changing views from the train windows, and my special new summer vacation comic book: a thicker edition that featured a puzzle page. The ride, filled with anticipation, seemed longer than what it had to have been.

The summer before, I had met Jules and Glenn. They were brothers—Glenn, the handsome, older brother; Jules, the bright and more precocious. Only a year or so separated any of us and we all played together. Every day of the summer, the fields and pine forests submitted to us and our revelry, we camped out, we hiked.

Once a week or so, we hiked up the Hoffman dirt road, all the way to the general store. I spent much of my time there admiring the display of Camper King pocketknives. My favorite was the knife with not two, not just a double blade, but no less than five blades for camping, including: a can opener, a bottle opener, a screwdriver, and an awl. Hopes of obtaining that knife propelled me through many quiet days, certainly up that hot Hoffman road to the general store.

We helped Old Man Schwartz on the farm. And at the end of the summer, as he had promised, Schwartz took us to the Lava Fire Department Fair. We had been looking forward to it for two months. There had been threats of "if you don't help out…" or "if you don't behave yourself, you won't go to the Lava Fair." But we did get to go, in Schwartz's black Ford pickup truck. And, it was great. We pitched pennies, threw wooden rings over bottle necks, ate ice cream and hot dogs, spent the dollar we each had saved, and walked through the heated August afternoon as it baked the final days of summer.

When it was over and we had to return to the city, we knew there was next year; we would see each other then. School would have come and gone and it would be summer again.

"Next summer….See you next summer!" It was waiting, off in the wings.

And now, at the depot in Narrowsburg, I recalled that depressing day, as I stood quietly at the top of that next summer, my mother and I, in the hot sun, in our city clothes, waiting for Schwartz, visions of Jules and Glenn romping in my head, the fun we'd have; summer was here. And around the turn, there came Schwartz's pickup. I could see him alight. I saw him bend slowly and lift our luggage onto the back of the truck. So, what was wrong? At once I knew.

"Are Jules and Glenn here?" I asked. Schwartz barely shook his head. So, I would have to wait for them? They hadn't arrived yet. I would have to spend a day or two alone. Not a pleasing prospect. I was ready for my friends. For the summer.

"They ain't comin'," Schwartz said.

"When? Today? This week?" I was confused. Why couldn't they be here today? Now!

"They ain't comin' this summer," Schwartz said, as he got in his truck. And one of the darkest clouds of my early life descended, enveloping me. I was left to contend with and resolve one of the most shocking and unexpected developments I could have imagined. My friends, whom I had anticipated for months, who had constituted summer, would not be coming. At all. "This summer," Schwartz said. I would be alone. It would be a different summer. It would be empty. Riding to the farmhouse, I felt betrayed, hurt, hopeless. Summer had come and gone in the few moments since Schwartz's pickup had arrived, and I was left with sadness. It was as if I had paid for something, taken it away, but on opening the package found it to be vacant. Jules and Glenn would not be coming up... at all. There would not be summer as it was last year. I was alone.

So that was it: the reason for the feelings of sadness as I thought back to that late June day at the train depot, as my mother and I awaited Schwartz's pickup; as what had promised to be a wonderful recap of a past summer collapsed and died.

It had taken more than two years before I went beyond the town of Narrowsburg into the hills of Cochecton and Lava to find Hoffman Road and Schwartz's farm.

I passed the old Lava firehouse and pulled over alongside a shoulder where a gray-haired man was mowing his lawn. He remembered the farm, Old Man Schwartz, and Schwartz' son Daniel, who was killed in the war. That had been a tragedy which had always hung over the farm in the years after the war. And he recalled the people who had stayed at the farm in the early fifties, the reason being his corner was where the postman—not wishing to negotiate the long dirt road to the farm—left the mail. The man's name was Kent. He said a little memorial to some of the old timers had been erected at the top of Hoffman Road.

As he had said, there in the brush, at the top of Hoffman Road, was a wooden table, a bench, and a plaque nailed to a tree with about two dozen names engraved on it. One name stood out. I had noticed a Skinner Road driving beyond Narrowsburg that afternoon. The name was familiar, of course. Skinner was Schwartz's good friend. Schwartz was forever going to see "Old Man Skinner" about something. Skinner, who was old in 1950, now, a half century later, had a road named after him; he was engraved on a plaque; a town father. I didn't see any other names I recognized, and I drove down the path.

I passed a large lot with a couple of trailers on it and not much more. Nothing appeared familiar, and I thought I must have gone astray. That was when I saw it. The old shed. It was where Schwartz kept his venerable Ford pickup. The shed had always been directly across from the farmhouse, with its concrete pillars and several steps leading to the house. But now, there was no house. The ancient edifice was gone. The shed stood alone, but it remained where it had always been.

It was difficult to believe, but dead ahead was where my mother had picked berries; off to my left and up the hill was the pine forest; to my right was the site of an old log fence where Jules, Glenn, a young girl named Carol, and I posed for a group picture. It was the afternoon I had gotten stung by a wasp.

Beyond the fence was a brook. I didn't see it, but traces of it had to exist somewhere. There were boulders and slabs of rock alongside of it and a giant oak with some low branches over the water, a few feet from the edge. Jules, Glenn, and I used to jump from the rocks to the branch and swing over the water, then jump back onto the rocks. It was quite a dare the first time we tried it, and a proud feat when each of us had accomplished it. Thereafter, that first summer, any newcomers to the group had to prove themselves by jumping from the rocks to the branch and back to the rocks again.

I was playing alone; Jules and Glenn were not there that second summer. I walked down to our haunt by the brook and stood on the jumping-off boulder, gazing a few feet away at the low-lying branch, inviting, over the water. No one was there now. It wasn't like last summer, but I could hear the chiding voices urging me up and out. I swung my arms, bounded up, and grabbed hold of the branch above the brook. I could still make it. Achievement. I felt free. I began my swing forward to increase momentum for the flight backward when I lost my grip and fell onto the flat rocks and water below. I lay there in a state of near shock. The wind had been knocked out of me, the water was cold, and I felt frightened. The jolt I got made me think I had broken myself. I was afraid to try and move. Could I have survived that kind of impact? Now, I thought, I had really done it. And who would find me? Who would know? I would have to get up; have to make it back. And what would my mother have to say?

I was fortunate. I had landed flat. I got up, and shaken by a considerable scare, I dripped my way back to the farmhouse. My mother didn't make more of a big deal out of it than just another case of a kid slipping on the edge of a rill and getting wet. But I knew, it all could have ended, stupidly, right there. Another inch. Another moment. Another rock. I had been very lucky.

So I stood at the spot, all these years later, looking for the brook. The bed was dried out. But the oak was there and the rocks were strewn about. And fifty years ago, a little boy swung a bit too zealously, almost did himself in, and got the fright of his life. No one saw it, no one knew, no one would ever know.

"Glenn and me"

"Jules"

"Schwartz's Pick-up truck"

"Mom"

"Dad and me in front of Schwartz's Farm. Narrowsburg, N.Y. 1949"

Highbridge

Jay Alper. The new kid...from Brooklyn. Short, cropped
black hair. A well-worn, light brown leather jacket. He
was proud of the jacket, rarely removed it. He was proud of
Brooklyn, and proudest of his two older brothers, particularly
Allan, closest in age to Jay, a Brooklyn College student.

Jay was twelve when he came to Washington Heights;
a time of change for many of us. We had just completed six
years of elementary school and a year of junior high school.
There seemed hardly time or space for new friends, from
different places far away, but Jay fit in quickly, effortlessly.
He was introspective, friendly, a decent athlete, not hostile,
but could hold his own in a tussle. He did not back away.
He was game. He laughed a lot. He was a good friend. And
it was from Jay that I first learned about arm wrestling (we
only had known about Indian wrestling); balancing on your
palms under your thighs, arms thrust between your legs,
hands flat against the sidewalk; or balancing using only

elbows against your knees, a first move on the way to a headstand. He knew lots of new stuff, from Brooklyn.

So when Jay suggested an afternoon at Highbridge Pool, I went with him. The only neighborhood swimming pool I had ever been to was Miramar Pool, a mile or so uptown from the 170s. Miramar was a relatively clean pool, bright and as nice as a city pool can be, with individual lockers and a refreshment bar. Highbridge was more than a mile south of the 170s, more alien territory than areas north of us, and in a neighborhood of Washington Heights which was becoming increasingly crowded and nasty. And, at eleven, I had only been to Miramar with adults. Jay and I were going to go to Highbridge alone. Reservations left me anxious, and in fact I did not really want to go; it seemed too much trouble, but...

We took bathing suits rolled in towels. I don't recall whether or not I told my mother where I was going, and we headed for Highbridge. Access to the pool was gained through a kind of community locker area. But there were no lockers. You got a steel mesh basket and an elastic bracelet with a number on it. Clothes were placed in the basket and given over to a man at a window. He stowed the basket on a shelf inside. You walked over the concrete locker room floor to the pool, with your bracelet and tag.

The swimming area seemed immense. Kids of every age and disposition were in the pool. It was so crowded most of the water was displaced by the crush of bodies. Swimming was not an option. It was more or less getting wet, getting bumped; finding yourself between players, not having the kind of solitary fun you might expect to have in a pool. Highbridge was host to the huddled masses, unhuddled.

There were no private games here, no unintruded-upon moments, no space, no calm. Thrust in amongst strangers who were simply happy to be wet, you took what you got: the crowd. And, having paid your money, and having checked your stuff, you hung in and waded across the afternoon to get through it.

We did get through it and, seeing how late it was becoming, we cavalierly made our way from the splash hole into the locker area. The relief I felt to be going home, however, suddenly gave way to shock and a terrible enervation. We were not the only ones in the area, just another two stragglers to claim their clothes. The chamber was filled with hundreds of pushing, screaming, jostling kids. There were several lines at each of at least a half dozen windows, but no clean division between the lines. It was one massive throng, with no hint as to where the ends of any line were to be found.

Jay and I simply stopped and commenced standing. The "lines" did not move. And although the scene was chaotic when we had arrived, within a half hour, hundreds had multiplied into thousands, chaos turned to frenzy, and enervation succumbed to hopelessness…and panic. Most of the pushers and shovers in our immediate space were older teens and many of them just bullied their way into the lines. Jay and I became dispensable bits of flotsam.

As we remained fixed on the filthy slime which coated the cold concrete floor, I noticed a short, somewhat disfigured man standing about five or six places before us on an adjacent line. One of the man's legs was horribly deformed, scarred, and considerably shorter than the other. It was the early 1950s and polio, not yet dealt the final blow,

71

was still a major summertime scare, with warnings about crowds, public pools, and lingering in wet, chilling bathing suits widely publicized. Each time this crippled man took a listing step, the warnings took on a new dimension; the scare became exponential. Our line, meanwhile, did not advance. The muddy slime became deeper. The crowd thickened.

At the front of the expansive room, near the wall of windows, a policeman stood. After waiting with Jay for more than an hour, I broke ranks and miraculously made my way to the officer. The surrounding boys, I told him, the gangsters and thugs on all sides, were impeding our progress, not letting us move up. I looked at the clock on the wall. It was after six. I was to have been home by five. We had left the pool sometime around four-thirty. The policeman's blank look before he answered was unforgettable, as were his words to me. He waited, until I was sure he would say nothing at all, almost as if he did not hear me. And then he said: "What do you want me to do?"

I lost Jay and was not able to rejoin the line anywhere other than at the very back of the room. There was no other course of action. Jay had been swallowed up in the crowd. There was no sign of him. So I stood once again...and stood, this time, by myself. I worried about getting the right clothes basket, not getting home at all that night, and polio. When I did get home, it was alone, after eight, and finding that my parents had called the police.

I don't recall discussing the episode with Jay during the next few years we went around together, but when he called me, a couple of generations later, he reminded me of a short story club we had both belonged to in junior high school. I thought of the Highbridge incident and told Jay I would try writing about it.

Almost one year after September 11, 2001, on a hot August afternoon, I had spent the better part of an hour on New York's Eleventh Avenue, waiting to get into the Lincoln Tunnel. The heat was sweltering, the traffic, at five in the afternoon, overwhelming. At last, as I was making the left turn onto the approach to the tunnel, a uniformed police officer jumped in front of my car and pointed an accusing finger at me, effectively halting my vehicle.

"You! Pull over!"

The turn was legal. I had just had my car properly inspected and registered. All tags were affixed and in place. I was not a fugitive. The plates were plainly visible. I was not inebriated, nor did I appear particularly menacing. I had courteously allowed the aggressive driver to my right to make the left before me and had been patiently awaiting my turn. I could not imagine why the officer was pointing at me as he barked his harsh words. I pulled over.

Carefully placing both hands on the steering wheel, I asked, "What did I do?"

"License and registration," he said. I complied.

Looking around, I saw the crush of vehicles vie for any place that would put them another foot closer to the mouth of the tunnel. I saw strange-looking men, at the end of a day's work, in unusual trucks and automotive contraptions, carrying heavy and unconventional-looking tools and machinery. No one else was stopped. But my car was white and a convertible. The officer disappeared into his car where he wrote out my infraction ticket. Nearly thirty minutes later, he appeared at my lowered window and gave me the seventy-dollar summons.

"What did I do?" I repeated.

"No seatbelt," he said.

Somehow, I thought, with not yet a year having passed since the horrific attack of September 11, our guardians and protectors would have better things to watch for and worry about at the mouth of the Lincoln Tunnel in New York at rush hour than seat belt infractions. I assumed most New Yorkers thought so. It was my deepest desire to convey that to the officer, but could only imagine him looking at me, with that familiar blank stare, saying: "What do you want me to do?"

Sid

There were Saturdays and vacation days when my best friend Ross and I walked east, from our street on Cabrini Boulevard, past Pinehurst and Fort Washington avenues to Broadway. But although, looking back, I often wonder where we were going, I vividly recall our route…as well as a strange character we invariably encountered along the way, a character I never forgot. Sid.

Most times, our jaunts to Broadway revolved around trips to one of the several candy stores on the strip. The nucleus of the call lay in finding and obtaining the latest issue of our favorite EC comic book: *Tales from the Crypt, Vault of Horror, Haunt of Fear,* or one of the two science fiction magazines: *Weird Fantasy* or *Weird Science.* And then there was the most recent and strangest of the EC family: *Mad*…before it became the popular magazine it is today. Those were the days, notably of Harvey Kurtzman, before his success in *Playboy* magazine with Little Annie Fanny; the days of Wally Wood and his incredibly shaded, sexy, sensual, and detailed feminine forms and faces; and Jack Davis, who went on to become one of America's leading commercial cartoonists. Those were the days of the brilliant artists Joe Orlando, Al Williamson, Jack Kamen, Al Feldstein, and Bill Severin. And, of course, publishing giant Bill Gaines. But not everyone appreciated the talents of these men, and there were those who objected to what they were publishing, even though "EC" stood for Entertainment Comics. I recall a precursor to what eventually happened to these comic books, a hint of what was to come when they were sued and banned by a righteous, what now would be called "politically correct" group of "concerned" adults.

During a bout with the flu, my father asked me if I wanted anything from the outside. I knew he would stop at a newsstand for the paper so I asked him to get one of the recent EC books. I provided him with a list in case my first choice was not available. Apparently it wasn't, and my father was compelled to recite the entire slate: *Crypt, Horror, Fear, Weird Science, Fantasy,* and *Mad.* The newsy, who carried none of the above and was also not as familiar with the titles as a local candy store man would be, asked my father what kind of little monster he had at home.

But Ross and I felt no such alienation at any of our familiar Broadway haunts. And so, before they were to disappear forever, as many good things do, after locating the object of our search on the colorful rack, we settled in, on one of the red plastic spinning stools and ordered egg-creams for seven cents, with pretzels, or if it was an especially hot afternoon, lime rickeys. And, on the black-and-white flecked marble countertop, we read the Crypt Keeper's latest tale. You could smell the new ink on the pages.

The chocolate sodas lasted for no more than one story and we needed to save something for that night at home. So, to buoy the enervation of departure and maintain our high spirits, we plunked down another nickel for a Three Musketeers bar on the way out of Dave's candy store, or just for serendipity's sake, purchased a box of Dick Tracy Candy and Toy (cartoons and story on back of package). Who knew what might have been in there? And, with fresh *Tales from the Crypt* rolled to protrude from our back pocket, we headed for home.

It could have been on the way to, or returning from, the candy store on Broadway that Ross and I almost invariably ran into Sid. I do not clearly remember the first time I had ever seen Sid, but it seemed like he had always been there, wandering up and down the block; just a part of the neighborhood, a fixture, particularly on 177th Street, where he lived.

Up until that year, I had never had any confrontation, dealings, or conversation with Sid. Now, however, things were changing. As we spent less time in the company of parents, and more hours alone and with mischievous pals, and as we felt urged to test our grit on this threshold of manhood, challenges presented themselves... everywhere. Sid was a challenge.

Sid was somewhere between fifty and sixty years old; it was difficult to tell. He was about six feet two or three, had gray hair worn in a crew cut, and was afflicted with some sort of spastic palsy. His face was somewhat contorted, his arms flailed about, his posture was stooped, and he was not especially understandable. Sometimes he drooled. Occasionally he would burst into a giraffe-like run as he came after us…most likely, playfully. We could not discern if Sid's affliction was primarily mental or physical. It seemed a large part of both, although we were never quite sure. There were two or three children in the neighborhood within a few years of our age group who had had cerebral palsy, so we were familiar with that, and we understood physical impairment need not affect mental faculties at all. Sid's condition, however, did not seem limited to cerebral palsy.

I don't recall how we knew his name. I suppose, in his garbled, inarticulate way, he may have told us. But we called him Sid, and he seemed to accept that. Whatever the case, we recognized the appellation and took instant heed when one of us called: "Here comes Sid!"

Usually the encounter took place between Broadway and Fort Washington Avenue, Sid's block. Sometimes, if we were on the other side of the street, given that Ross was in a particularly daring and frisky frame of mind, I can recall my friend initiating the meet by, contrary to all common sense, yelling: "Hey, Sid!" There were occasions, if excessive enthusiasm was demonstrated by Sid, when, a bit spooked, we did not follow through and left poor Sid in his giraffe-like pursuit of us. But there were those instances when Ross crossed the street, and engaged Sid in what appeared to pass for conversation, however nonsensical or pointless.

It was during one such "conversation" that Sid alluded to his FBI badges. And in several subsequent "conversations" invited us to come up to his apartment to see the collection. I had had another friend who was at that time quite taken with the FBI and who was also invited by Sid to view the collection. In his slurred and distorted enthusiasm, Sid swore to us that he had been an FBI agent, and tried to prevail upon us to view the proof… "upstairs." We thought a lot about that and were sorely tempted to venture up…just to see. But we never quite dared.

It wasn't clear whether Sid lived alone or with some guardian or caretaker. He was never with anyone but always alone on the street. The times were rare, however, when Ross and I could walk the block between Fort Washington and Broadway and not run into, or run away from, Sid. If he saw us, he ran after us with the kind of urgency that could only indicate the necessity to communicate a message of extreme importance. And sometimes we indulged his apparent exigency. Sometimes we ran out of his reach.

We often wondered if Sid, or a part of him, was for real, just wanted to play, or whether there was something darker lurking within, but Ross and I had met one of the rites of passage, almost. I left Washington Heights in 1958 and never got to see Sid again. I suppose I left him there, in the Heights. But I did take with me that forever to remain unseen, gleaming and venerable collection of badges. Proof positive of Sid's FBI days.

AUTUMN

The Park

The southernmost boundary of my early life in Washington Heights, in terms of both time as well as space, was the J. Hood Wright Park, between Haven Avenue overlooking the Hudson River and Fort Washington Avenue. It was better known as "the park." No one ever called it by its formal name. I look upon my northernmost boundary as the RKO Coliseum movie theater on Broadway at 181st Street.

My earliest recollections of being in the park were of Saturday afternoons, waiting for my mother, while in the care of my grandmother. After working a half day, my mother would meet us a convenient distance from the downtown exit of the 175th Street A train. I can remember walking from the 176th Street ramp toward the center of the park, near the little cake house, as my grandmother would point and say, "There she is." And there she would be; in her three-quarter-length woolen jacket with her multicolor paisley wool blend scarf around the collar or protruding from the pocket. Very smiley, arms outstretched. I was three years old. I ran.

Some years later I tangled with the class terror, Joseph Finger, on a grassy park hill, and pinned him; a major and surprising triumph for me. But, as he protested, he was on roller skates. Two years later, an older boy with exceptionally dark and heavy eyebrows which grew together tore my yellow pea shooter from my hand and made a swift getaway as he ducked through the space between strands of double wire that connected waist-high iron posts enclosing a grassy quadrangle in the center of the park. My father was very angry with me for letting that happen, although the pea shooter was only five cents. I never forgot it. That nickel bought a lot of memories.

The J. Hood Wright Park across from the school, P.S. 173 on Fort Washington Avenue, was an oasis. It was divided in two main parts and featured chess and checker tables at the cusp of the western end, and a sprinkler pool and playground on the eastern side. The playground boasted swings, slides, a jungle gym (which we called monkey bars), and a see-saw. Dead center of the park was an indoor recreation building, and at its northern end was a large ball field, complete with horizontal and parallel bars.

But my favorite place in the entire park was the little green, pointy-topped, cake house…although "cake" was not the sole refreshment offered there. It was run by a wonderful woman known as Mrs. Downey. Her name was considered interchangeable with Miss Downey during the chaotic and thirsty moments trying to catch her attention. She wore a white apron with green trim and a green-and-white smock. Her hair was an artificially curled and colored brown, showing gray streaks, and she was sometimes assisted by her adult son or one of the older, (far older than us) teenaged kids. My friend Lawrence called Mrs. Downey, Mrs. Uppey. He thought that was extremely funny, and threw himself into spasms of laughter each time he used the name.

Among the treats to be had at Mrs. Downey's were Mello-Rolls, a creamy cylinder of ice cream made to pre-fit a specially shaped cone (it wasn't conical at all), two kinds of pretzels, the round twists and the long straights which discerning customers knew tasted differently, and beyond the common colas, real kid sodas like sarsaparilla, cream soda, root beer, and RC. She also sold Popsicle Pete twin ice pops that could be broken through the wrapper to share, although this left the dilemma of who got the prize-worthy bag. Or if you preferred real ice cream on the stick, Mrs. Downey sold chocolate-dipped vanilla, covered with a white, blue, and red paper bag. In a separate class were the Bryers Dixie cups of chocolate and vanilla whose lids could be peeled to reveal fresh, clean, blue, brown, or black and white photos of movie stars, cowboys or athletes. With any change one might have had left, two- and three-cent variety candy included intriguing wax bottles in various shapes, my favorite being a tiny canteen, which could be bitten into and chewed after the sweet and colored liquid was sucked out of it. One last item worth mentioning, because Mrs. Downey was always sold out of it, and because for some reason one can rarely get it anywhere today, was the frozen Milky Way…on a stick.

In the spring, when school was out, and certainly during the summer, there was never less than a crowd of screaming kids at Mrs. Downey's two gaping wooden windows; everyone simultaneously yelling the woman's name, except for Lawrence. Lawrence yelled, "Mrs. Uppey, Mrs. Uppey," sending himself into paroxysms of convulsive laughter.

There was something for everyone in J. Hood Wright, and very few days in the nice weather, after school, when the routes home—no matter how long those were—did not take us through the park. Lawrence and I did it together, dressed in our school clothes. Then he moved away.

Rarely did one travel north of the Coliseum. There was no need. Everything from department stores, like Wertheimers to the Horn & Hardart Automat, F.W. Woolworth and four more movie houses could be accessed by walking east for just a few blocks on 181st Street. Men's clothing stores like Bonds, Ripley, Crawford, and Howard Clothes, long-gone candy and chocolate shops like Loft, Gregor, and Fanny Farmer, as well as shoe stores, hat stores, haberdashery, and eating establishments abounded for the shopper or for the amusement of the casual stroller and passer-by. There was the elegant St. James Restaurant and Nick's Ice Cream Parlor and Soda Fountain. But the heart of the street was the exciting RKO Coliseum, for through its doors, worlds, and travel to those worlds, were unlimited.

Dick Tracy came alive for me in 1947 in the person of Ralph Byrd dealing with a frightening character called the Claw, and Kirk Allen—to my delightful surprise—appeared on the screen in a Superman serial around the same time only to give way to a "to be continued" notice after about fifteen incredible minutes. I never learned what happened. But Superman lived once upon a Saturday morning at the RKO Coliseum.

In 1951, there was much promotion heralding the coming of a movie called *The Thing*. Markings were emblazoned on curbs and in streets leading to the Coliseum, posters were hung, bills were posted. There were flyers, stills, handbills, word of mouth.

No one knew exactly what *The Thing* was. One could only speculate...and anticipate. On the exciting opening night, the theater filled with jabbering children made it difficult to discern much dialogue, but that was hardly necessary. Neither did the white-uniformed matrons shining their flashlights across aisles improve the noise levels. The giant carrot, or whatever it was, never showed itself and seemed to pose not much of a threat in the end. The real nightmare of the evening was in trying to follow or even hear the first film of the double feature that night. It was *The Lavender Hill Mob* with Alec Guinness and Stanley Holloway, a sophisticated British comedy, but painfully, obviously, not what the audience had come to see...or hear. The resulting din was indescribable. It rendered the film's showing, for its eighty-some odd minutes on the screen, one of world history's lost performances. And what were those little gold Eiffel Towers all about anyway?

My mother occasionally took me to the Coliseum. One of the highlights of those days was the treat of a Nedicks hot dog for a dime and a small orange drink for a nickel. Nouvelle cuisine could not hope to compete. The snack, at the Nedicks, diagonally across the street from the movie house, usually came after the show.

On this particular Sunday, my mother wore her multicolored paisley wool blend scarf. Somehow, she misplaced it, and it was not until we were outside that the scarf was missed. We got back into the Coliseum and a superficial search was made with the aid of an usher's light and probably in the wrong row. No one had turned it in. It was not found. When we left the theater, for the second time, I had a terrible sense of loss. I had shared the afternoon; somehow, I felt, I shared responsibility for the loss as well. My mother still took me for the frankfurter and the small orange drink. But all the way home, I kept thinking of the scarf, hoping it might turn up.

In the mid-seventies I would periodically take the number 4 Madison Avenue bus just to visit Washington Heights. The neighborhood had changed considerably. There wasn't much to see. After walking up and down Broadway and visiting my old street, in hopes of seeing one or two familiar faces, I walked through the park to the bus stop on Fort Washington Avenue. It was getting cold and I had not seen one face I knew. Everyone, I supposed, had left the old neighborhood. It seemed clear no one of the old crowd remained in what was now a changed place.

Then, as I waited for the bus at the entrance to the park, a young man in the company of two elderly people walked slowly onto the avenue. The three of them perhaps had just had a quiet, although chilly, stroll through the park. The younger man's face looked ashen. I recognized him as one of the older kids who used to help out Mrs. Downey during the summers. I could recall him sipping a cream soda from within the little cake house as he waited on customers. It impressed me then as being one of the privileged benefits of working for Mrs. Downey. He had aged. The older man and woman, evidently his parents, had a grayish cast to their appearance. Apparently they never left the Heights; never made it out; did not move forward. I boarded my bus and decided then I no longer resided in Washington Heights but lived elsewhere.

About two decades later, my wife and I were moving my mother into a senior residence in Riverdale. We had occasion to drive up Broadway, through Washington Heights, and passed the corner at Broadway and 181st Street. I looked for the RKO Coliseum, but it was not there. The movie theater was not there, the building was not there, even the corner's configuration was unrecognizable. Nedicks was not there.

As we headed north, I wondered whatever became of the paisley scarf. It was lost, as lost as it ever was or would be. But I had the distinct feeling it was out there somewhere. Curiously, I no longer had a sense of loss, certainly less than on the day it vanished. And I felt good about that.

P.S. 173

When I think of P.S. 173, names come to mind. Lawrence Landis, Richard Feare, Enrique Chaffarday. And the captains: Arnold Alperin, Jerome Albenberg, Ronald Ettus.

The pristine red brick building comes to mind as well; with the white faux marble stairs in front of the school, (the stairs rarely used by anyone, save those who were kept well after three o'clock, when the side exit doors had long been locked) and the shiny brass handrails that we polished by sliding upon them when we did use the center doors. I can still smell the brass.

That pretty picture of the school was taken from 173's early years in the 1940s. By the late 60s and 1970s the school—at least its appearance—had gone to seed and was covered by graffiti, as was much of Washington Heights. And it had aged, melting into the years, into deterioration; into, not so much encroaching time, but the encroaching times. But the memories of the early days and the early people remained. And they are unchanging, immutable.

Miss Callanan's first grade class was not all that pleasant. We folded our yellow pulpy papers and filled in the top two folds with our name, the date, our class, and the subject. Arithmetic papers were folded into four boxes, spelling papers only once in half, to form two columns. We knew what kind of lesson or test was to come based on how we were instructed to fold our papers. And the ink, spraying from those horrid pens when the nub got momentarily hung up in the paper's pulp…added mess to misery. If you were left-handed, all the worse. Of course, I was left-handed.

Tensions heightened when papers were "handed back." The grade you received was one of two—a cross: not good; a check: good. It was Lawrence Landis, seated one aisle to my left, who showed me how to successfully defuse this tension as well as mollify the devastating effects of a possible poor grade. Landis, a comfort, a smile and a fellow traveler, seemed to know how to make light of an otherwise difficult half hour. What he did was fold his returned paper lengthwise in four, then fold the bottom inch toward him, the next inch segment away, making a zigzag pattern, until the entire paper was transformed into an inch square packet. He would then hold the little square, pressing it on his desktop with an index finger, letting go all at once, as it sprang up, revealing itself as a nifty Jack-in-the-Box: an improvised toy; an entertainment; an amusement, fashioned out of the very cruel weaponry the adult world was using to torture us. With judicious use of this toy, the feeling was that we had prevailed.

We did not always prevail. In fact, it was rare. And when we did prevail, we did not always triumph. In second grade, I met Enrique. Enrique was a "new boy." He came from Ecuador and spoke no English. The frustration showed, although none of us understood just what it was that made Enrique so bellicose. He clowned, he lashed out; he fought. And soon Enrique enjoyed the designation "toughest kid in the class." He was feared because he communicated on a physical level. There was no verbal level. None of us spoke Spanish, and this much he knew. So Enrique kept a scowl on his expression in his guarded isolation.

His world was unique. I recall watching him fondle a grayish ball, rolling it between his palms one day. Occasionally he would take a small nip at it. At first he refused to tell me what it was, but with annoying persistence I eventually learned it was something I had never heard of before called Turkish Taffy. He savored it. When I located the stuff for a nickel on a candy stand, I was surprised to find it was flat, not a ball, and pure white, not gray. Of course, how Enrique created his taffy ball remains a mystery.

Love of Turkish Taffy, however, was not sufficient grounds for camaraderie between Enrique and me. He had several disruptive incidents in class, enough of them for me to consider him fair game as the bad guy when he tripped me one morning, and I shoved back at him. He slipped and fell against one of our fastened-to-the-floor desks, hitting his eyebrow on the corner. His skin split and he bled. It had been a short tussle and hardly a fight, but I felt I had won it, whatever it was. I don't recall that I even bothered to point out the whole thing was an accident in that Enrique had slipped. I simply had beaten the bully. Anyway, he had started it. But had anyone seen that? I was to learn this did not seem to matter. Not to the teacher; worst of all, not to my classmates. Enrique was on his way to the nurse with blood coming from the area around his eye. I had never drawn blood before. What a victory. But, suddenly I was a pariah.

The girls refused to speak to me. I was scorned. Accused. It took what seemed like hours for the finger pointing to stop. Then Enrique came back to class with a big bandage over his eyebrow and it started all over again. And the stigma lasted for days; until the thing, his bandage, came off. Even then, Enrique's little scar served as a reminder of the mishap and my misdeed. Thereafter, I was always to remember how quickly sympathies can turn; how fickle are the sentiments of the group. A few weeks later Enrique gradually became known as Henry.

As the days of tests, papers and homework dragged on there were those in the great out-there, somewhere behind the curtain, who championed the survival of the suffering school boy and girl (mostly, somehow, it was the boy). On the radio, they called us: "fellows and girls" or "gang." To the bubble gum companies we were sometimes "Hey kids!" (Although I never knew a girl who listened to Superman or Captain Midnight or Tom Mix, or who collected Indian cards.)

The Goudey Gum Company was printing a series of Indian gum cards. They were colorful, collectible, tradable, flippable, and in short, for many days, my reason for living. One afternoon, however, life nearly came to an end. As I was admiring my stash of mint Goudey Indian cards, including Geronimo, Powhatan, Simon Girty, and the recently acquired Captain John Smith; as I was reviewing and considering the exploits of Jim Bridger and Colonel Bowie and admiring the majestic stance of the Indian on the Sioux Tribe card with its fresh, red background, some of the most feared words ever heard in any class reverberated through the room. There were two key phrases. The first presaged the second: "What do you have there?" It signaled the coming of the more ominous: "Bring those up here, now!" That was the killer. There was no option but to comply. The youngster, embarrassed, was shamed before all. His treasures were confiscated. And then came the final directive: "Sit down, please!" The reluctance to sit must have appeared obvious, for how could one have stayed seated when one's pockets were so many ounces lighter? So, shocked, chagrined, I remained standing.

"Did you hear me, young man? Take your seat." Only then did I sit. But before being fully seated, one thought flooded my mind: retrieval; how to get to her drawer; how to get back into the room when this bad school day was over; how to regain property rightfully mine; how to restore my very soul.

My friend Gary, perhaps because we shared a relatively uncommon name, as well as wads of endangered Goudey Indians, seemed also to share the indignity I suffered. We trekked to the 181st Street five-and-dime, also known as F.W. Woolworth, sought out the hardware section and, for a mere dime, purchased two skeleton keys, one with, and one without a notch at the end of its shaft. My keys to retrieval.

The two of us, on the following day, lagged behind at dismissal time, quickly backtracked to the now-deserted floor and our locked room, and tried the keys. The notched one worked. Exhilaration. And the desk drawer was unlocked. The packet of Indians lay there, rubber banded, atop notes and paper scraps, abandoned but waiting to be reclaimed. I seized them, restoring my life and self-regard. We closed the drawer and left the room. Gary and I uttered a chortle of glee, flew down the stairwell, and left the school. Redemption. Beyond that, the euphoria of success. Mrs.

Bouton, our third grade teacher, never missed the Indians. For me, it was the highlight of that year.

Since the first grade, classrooms were typically divided into three sections, probably for the teacher to subtly discern between bright, average, and dull students. The division, however, was not particularly deceptive. It was, in fact, transparent, and perhaps, sadly, not only to those in section one.

For as long as I can recall, Richard Feare sat in section three. He was a small, dark-haired, quiet boy with few friends, but not necessarily unintelligent. Slow perhaps, his banishment each year to section three might have been due in part to a certain dullness he evinced. When the teacher left the room for a moment, and the class was quick to combust into a frenzy of chaos, Richard would sit with his hands folded on his desk. He may have been the only one. Perhaps because he had no friends to talk with, he rarely talked. Wherever his mind roamed, it did not seem to be anywhere in earshot of questions from the front of the room, for he never had any answers. On occasion, our teacher threatened a member of another section with: "Would you like to sit next to Richard?" And some of his classmates may have laughed.

It was on a late spring afternoon in May when the trees lining the residential streets of Fort Washington Avenue were turning green with new buds. School was out, summer was on its way, and the kids who lived north of P.S. 173 formed a long column in disarray on their way home. The post-three o'clock elation and the headiness of dismissal on this balmy day was breezing the lot of us into the carefree late afternoon, past Richard Feare's place, a ground-floor dwelling in an apartment building, off the street. The moment would not have been notable. And the spot would not have been remarkable. It would have been as it was on any other day, standing beyond the shade of the trees and stopping the sunshine on its own, but for a crowd on the sidewalk around the door of the Feare apartment. In the street was a large white ambulance with all its sharp, terrifying markings. Its rear doors gaped to reveal shelves, canisters, and frightening equipment.

Richard had not yet arrived home, but was only moments away. He appeared in time to see the attendants leaving his apartment carrying the stretcher with his mother on it. He ran up to the onlookers and burst into a torrent of tears, then stood, obedient, but trembling, as one or two from the crowd spoke to him, as his mother was lifted through the ambulance doors.

The word spread quickly, finding its way to the ears of eight-year-olds: Richard's mother had suffered a heart attack. In time, she came back home, but since that afternoon, there was something different about Richard. Something had changed about that block, about balmy spring afternoons, about mothers, about our expectation of the carefree, easy flow of events. About unimpeded fun.

There were heroes among us of whom we became aware in the later grades. And most of them were elected to the offices of safety patrol chieftains. The five top posts were first and second lieutenants, secretary, assistant captain, and captain of patrol. Those who ran for the positions generally arose from the ranks of the athletes, the scholarly, the good-looking or the tall. Any two of these traits virtually assured a successful run. But at least one was a requirement.

In my fourth grade year, the captain of patrol was Arnold Alperin, a tall, bright, and good-looking redheaded fellow. I told his little brother, Lewis, I envied him for having such a brother, me having no siblings with whom to cavort or look up to. Lewis told me he hated his brother. I didn't understand this and continued to be vaguely aware and admiring of Arnold's exploits around the neighborhood in subsequent years. He seemed unique. I had never, for example, heard of anyone in Washington Heights, much less a young person, being anything other than a Democrat. Arnold proclaimed himself a Republican. On Saturday nights, he would run through the local candy store where I worked, to the phone booths at the rear, to make what seemed a series of important phone calls. He flashed an address book, filled no doubt with dates and girls' numbers. Then he would rush out. On the way to and from the phones, he exchanged savvy quips with the candy store owners, for whom he had worked a year before, and made them laugh. Always clever, he had the attitude of "been there, graduated, done that," seemed always to have urgent business, and was never less than in a hurry. I only watched. One day, Arnold showed up at the candy store in his navy uniform. Years later, I heard he worked for Internal Revenue. His brother told me he still didn't like him.

Jerome Albenberg became captain of patrol the following year. He was short, but possessed unusual good looks, was very bright, and an extraordinary athlete.

An uncommonly sexy girl named Lenore, who was a year older than Jerome and several inches taller, lived on Pinehurst Avenue, a block from me. I had taken note of Lenore, and during the longer daylight savings evenings of May and June, rushed through suppers to run downstairs, not so much for the games of slug and errors, but to catch a glimpse of, perhaps exchange a few words with, Lenore. The exchanges were brief. I learned that although Lenore was outside nearly every night, she was waiting for Jerome, who traveled from a few blocks away and whose visits were rare. When he did appear, however, his ball playing prowess and coordination were impressive and nearly flawless. Lenore took note. She sat staring at him with her face cupped in her hands. Everyone marveled but Jerome. He already knew about the gifts he possessed. Good looking, bright, athletic, and captain of patrol. I reflected on there being little hope. But the next year, I ran for the office of captain of patrol.

It worked like this: Six boys ran. There were five offices. Most votes got the highest office. Next highest number of votes got the next highest office, and so on. Least number of votes lost out completely; got to be captain of an exit. We stood before the electorate as the votes were tallied. The six of us. I received the least number. It was the most embarrassing moment of my life. I cried. I wasn't Jerome, I wasn't Arnold, I wasn't athletic, I wasn't tall. But I got to be captain of an exit.

The guy who did become captain that year was Ronald Ettus. Not tall, but bright, good looking, an exceptional athlete, and a genuinely nice person. Ettus had one of those unusual relationships with a ball. It would always seek him out to rest snugly in his glove or find the sweet spot on his bat. He could pluck it out of the air despite the heights from which it alighted, and could stop it with his bat despite the speeds at which it traveled. He became a teacher. I met him on a subway platform some years later. Completely fascinated, he seemed taken with the virtues and wonders of tennis.

99

Sometime in 1946, Tom Mix and the Ralston Purina Company offered an interesting premium. For a thin dime and box top from Shredded Ralston, you got a neat little adjustable ring which enabled the wearer to look around corners. I got it. After weeks of waiting, which of course seemed like months, it came in a little brown envelope, addressed to me. I was slow to finish the cereal, however.

Rings that followed included Sky King's Gold Ore Ring, Magna-Glo-Writing Ring, and Navajo Treasure Ring, (for which one had to consume Peter Pan peanut butter) and a host of Lone Ranger rings, including the Flashlight Ring, the Six Shooter Ring, and the Weather Ring, which required proof of purchase of either Kix or Cheerios cereal. Always, however, I was slow to finish the cereal. And it was because of this sluggishness and limited cupboard space that I failed to acquire what for me became the ring of rings: The Lone Ranger Atom Bomb Ring. My mother simply refused to harvest any more fractionally-consumed boxes of cereal. One day, however, in Mrs. Storm's sixth grade class, my dreams were answered. Almost.

I don't remember who, but one of the boys—whom I thought was the luckiest kid in the room that day—flashed the ring. The Lone Ranger Atom Bomb Ring. It had been around for a couple of years, but I had never seen it, never held it, much less removed the rear fins to peer into the innards of the bomb itself and thereby witness the mini-phosphorescent atom bomb devastation. But the kid wouldn't let me see it. He would not let me hold it. I negotiated for the ring all day and finally assumed ownership of the coveted piece by day's end…after trading away a goodly proportion of my pockets' contents, trading cards, pen knives, pin backs, and do-dads.

My curiosity—although only moments remained until the final dismissal bell of the day—was not to be contained. I removed the fins and looked into the ring. Nothing. I adjusted the angle and cupped my hand over it to block out the light. It was then I heard those ominous words again.

"What do you have there? Bring that up here, please!"

She took the ring…and threw it in the wicker wastebasket just as the bell rang, signaling the end of the school day. And my atom bomb ring dream.

"Line up, in twos!"

The door was held open by the door monitor. We marched out. It was not the highlight of this day. And not until some forty years later did I get to look into one of these rings. But by then the little flecks of phosphorus had long since lost their ability to absorb light and had died.

Around that time I passed a sign in the seventies on Manhattan's east side that said Lawrence Landis, Real Estate. I made note of it and called him. We chatted for a bit. Essentially, he was somewhat perplexed as to why I called. I suggested lunch. He declined and indicated he was very busy these days.

After several weeks, I was driving past his office and decided to say hello in the wake of all the years. Someone was pulling his car out of a space just alongside of Lawrence's office. I pulled in.

"Mr. Landis in?" I asked the receptionist.

"Do you have an appointment?" she said.

"Just tell him his old buddy Gary from P.S.173 is here," I said. She rose and went into Landis' office. Moments later, she returned.

"I'm sorry," she said, "he's tied up. Would you care to make an appointment?"

"No. That's all right," I said. "Thanks." And I left.

I went out and stepped over to my car. There was a $115 dollar ticket on the windshield. I removed it and got into the car. I put the key into the ignition and turned it. Then I folded the ticket in half lengthwise, and again. I took the bottom inch and folded it toward myself and the next inch or so away, making a little, zigzag, Jack-In-The-Box. Then I pressed the packet on the dashboard, holding it down with my index finger for a moment. And I let it go.

Harriet

I couldn't have been more than seven or eight years old when I first laid eyes on Harriet. She, however, never quite saw me. Instantly, and forever more, she established the criteria for what it took to set The Heart Throb in motion. One might have termed it crush at first sight. But although the crush was not unique to me, (there were others) from what I can recall of <u>my</u> case of the fever, a few degrees of heat lingered for a mere fifty years. Or to keep the metaphor consistent, my "crush" left traces in my system of several reverberating aftershocks over time.

The neatly-clad and astonishing little redhead graced our fourth grade classroom long enough to chronically distract me from more serious pursuits, like schoolwork. Assembling in the schoolyard, lining up, entering class, sitting down, reciting or performing in any way became little more than exercises in watching for Harriet, standing tall before her, trying to catch her attention, seeking out her approval. None of it seemed to work, and too many days were spent gawking at her and freezing, motionless, into a disembodied heartbeat each time she talked, gestured or entered a room. I can still see her blue eyes.

It was on a late spring day, deceptively like summer and tantalizingly so, that I was moved to action. Joyce Roth was one of the higher intellects in our class, though not on the Harriet heartthrob level, and one of Harriet's better friends. Moreover, she was amicable, understanding, and approachable. So I approached Joyce. Did she think Harriet liked me? Would she find out? The day was torn by my impatience and laced with anticipation. Periodically, I scanned Joyce's aisle for a sign, sought encouragement at recess, passed reminder notes when possible. But Joyce was responsible and not likely to forget to inquire on my behalf. She was to meet me after school at three o'clock, at the school's south exit on West 173rd street.

The day was still beautiful and the weather warm, but I was warmer and did not share in the day's tranquility. In fact, what little remained of that afternoon was an indelible pain and disappointment. There was Joyce, waiting. My heart leapt. I approached her.

"Does Harriet like me?"

"No. Harriet says she doesn't like you."

"Why?" I asked, clinging to some hope for specious reasons that I might use to cushion my decimation.

"She says your ears stick out."

Devastated beyond ruin and somewhat numbed by this new revelation, I hurried home to investigate the matter further. Dashing upstairs, I took a position before my mother's full-length mirror. Standing close to it, I scrutinized my ears, staring at them and examining the distance at which they stood out from my head. They seemed all right and not particularly alien, although the longer I contemplated the protrusions, the stranger they became. It was at that point my mother came into the room.

"What are you doing, dear?" she asked.

"Do my ears stick out?" I moaned, anxious now for this final pronouncement, one that would hopefully mollify and rightfully spurn the derision I had suffered. A mother's inviolable truth.

"Well," she said, "just a little, dear." Alas, she was too truthful.

So the remainder of fourth grade passed as I shrunk from Harriet and could only stare longingly, but from safe distances, at her, hoping with the coming and going of the summer months that I might grow taller and stronger and that my ears might somehow retreat closer to the sides of my head.

It was a little more than a year later I awoke one Sunday morning with the brilliant idea of dressing and sneaking out of our apartment at the outrageously early hour, for me, of nine o'clock. I dressed carefully in what I thought were my most dashing clothes. The jersey was a tight one, showing off what semblance of a build I had. My trousers were creased; my jacket was air force bomber style with manly shoulders. My mission was to traverse J. Hood Wright Park on 176th Street and Pinehurst Avenue to emerge on Fort Washington Avenue at 173rd Street, just a few short blocks from where Harriet and her family lived.

I made my way briskly up to Pinehurst Avenue from Cabrini Boulevard and over to the park entrance ramp at 176th Street. There I paused, as my heart beat strongly in anticipation, as I bravely surveyed the park beyond. Hannibal before the Alps. The great Sunday morning adventure lay ahead. I was ready.

With the somewhat soothing consolation of "what could happen?" I forged ahead, traversing the park. What were the chances, I speculated, of my catching a glimpse of her? What were the chances of her being up at this hour? Of her going out? Of her seeing me? What were the chances of her noticing me…if she <u>was</u> up, if she did go out, if she did see me? Despite all odds, I pressed on, slicing through doubt and fear, marshalling hope, mobilizing energies, mustering determination, cutting through the early morning freshness and chill, as I half-hoped I somehow would miss her altogether.

Emerging somewhat more slowly and cautiously than I had entering the park, I looked about as if all of Fort Washington Avenue had been alerted of my arrival. I felt as though I were something of an intruder in the neighborhood. It was really a bit distant from my own. Yes, I attended school here, but as a resident with a support group of friends and neighbors, I was a foreigner. Hands in jacket pockets, I whistled my way toward Harriet's apartment building at 250 Fort Washington Avenue. Even the number of her address was tinged with romance, excitement, adventure, and danger. I waited.

And I waited. At first, I waited from across the street. Then, as the morning wore on, from in front of the building, before the short flight of steps. At one point, I can remember going up and inside the lobby. Perhaps that might draw her out. It did not. Others came and went. People looked at the young boy and may have wondered what the stranger was doing. For whom he waited. Each outward thrust of the heavy wrought iron and glass lobby door gave a start, blowing a little hope my way from the darkish lobby, ushering forth the chance, the possibility of the morning's adventure bearing some fruit. I waited the morning away until I got cold and tired. She never came down.

Shortly following the start of what then was known as junior high school, Harriet moved away, somewhere in or near an area called Forest Hills. I spent the next five years or so not thinking of her.

Somewhere ankle-deep into my sophomore year in college, while leafing through an old address book on a particularly desperate, date-deprived Saturday evening, I found her name. I cannot imagine how I came to procure her Forest Hills telephone number, but there it was. I studied it. I contemplated it. I dismissed it. I allowed it to challenge me. I let it simmer.

I suppose I was feeling lots better about myself during these college days than I had during my younger days at P.S. 173. After all, I was president of my sophomore class now, Grand Regent of my fraternity; I had succeeded in achieving a surprisingly good first year index, I had enjoyed a role—although a minor one—in a campus theater production, and, or so I thought, my ears didn't stick out...as much anyway. Not noticeably. So I called her number. And my voice had deepened. After several rings, Harriet answered the phone. I still recognized her voice. It had a kind of clipped sneer to it.

"Hi," I began cleverly. "You may not remember me. Gary…from your fourth, fifth, and sixth grade class in P.S. 173?"

"I'm afraid not," she said. There was no hesitation, no doubt in her voice. Same clipped sneer.

"I lived in Joanie Miller's building on Cabrini Boulevard? I was Joyce Roth's friend." Joan Miller was a good friend of hers. She sometimes visited Joanie. I had lived for those rare afternoons.

"Look, it's been a long time, and I really don't remember you at all."

Well, it really hadn't been that long a time, and those were very formative years for all of us. I thought we had been kind of an item; at least so far as classmates' teasing and rumors counted. I couldn't believe her not remembering at all.

"And Evelyn Strawlberg? Don't you remember the time someone stole your blouse at Evelyn Strawlberg's house at that little costume party and you had to leave in a borrowed pea coat?"

"I'm sorry," she clipped out, "I don't remember any of this. And I really don't have time to talk. I'm going out."

"You once said my ears stuck out."

And she hung up.

It took me awhile to forget that conversation and a while to regain some of the old sophomore confidence. I did not, however, risk another phone call to Harriet.

Some years passed, and I found myself broad
on a 50,000-watt radio station in Boston, Massac
I was performing an afternoon program, spinning records
and telling little stories. One of these vignettes was about
Harriet. It may have been the Joyce Roth debacle or the
try at getting a dinner date disaster. I always ended my
programs with the humble phrase: "I await your phone calls
in the outer lobby." No sooner had I uttered this phrase and
signed off, I was informed that I indeed had a call…in the
outer lobby.

The call was from a guy I didn't know. Nor did the guy
know me. But he had been listening to the show as he was
driving across Massachusetts into Boston. He had heard
the Harriet anecdote and said he almost drove off the road.
It seems his brother, he told me, was engaged to Harriet
but he—the caller—had been infatuated with her. "Who
wasn't?" he said. "And," he confided, "I knew exactly what
you meant when you described her. What a bitch!"

When I left Boston for New York, I was in my thirties
and found myself running into people I had known years
ago. They were mostly school chums from Washington
Heights, some High School of Music and Art people, and
even college pals. It was not unusual since everybody, at
one time or another, seems to gravitate to New York City.
But, as I told an old friend of mine: "Funny. I never ran into
Harriet."

When I nostalgically confessed this, my friend
counseled "You can't go home again!" and advised me to
hope I never see Harriet, because I would be sure to be
deeply disappointed. "Better," he said, "to remember her as
she was. That little redheaded beauty with the sharp blue

eyes. By now," he added sagely, "she is probably fat, old, and dumpy. You had best stay with your fantasies."

More and more of my time was taken with freelance narration work, which afforded me some freedom and took me far and wide during the course of a week. At one point, I contracted for a series of jobs in Douglaston, Queens. It was a bit of a trek, but I always harbored the thought of possibly running into Harriet, serendipitously, against the odds, despite my friend's admonition.

Then, one day, it happened. I was taken completely by surprise. Ascending a long flight of stairs at New York's Penn Station, tired and on my way home from an arduous day in Douglaston, I noticed a comely redhead some several steps ahead of me. She was dressed in a neat topper, just short enough to sport a shapely pair of legs. She was one of the few women in heels, a conservative pair of black pumps, and walked with a confident, unhurried pace. It couldn't be, I thought, but the closer I drew to her, the more this vision seemed to fit my expectations of what Harriet might look like now. She appeared, from the back, to be about the same age and height, as far as my recollections went. My scheme was to cunningly dash ahead and check her from the front. Surely, however, the entire effort rested on a wishful thought that I was mistaken.

Only a few smoothly executed steps taken two and three at a time, and I had arrived well in front of the woman. Artfully, I turned about and saw her face. It was her. But she didn't appear as my friend had predicted. She wasn't old, or fat or unrecognizably smothered by the years. She was lovely, radiant, and she sparkled, beyond expectations. Predictions were wrong. And now, in point of actual fact, it

<u>had</u> happened. The law of averages had worked out. There she was, walking toward me.

Feigning surprise with just the right measure of confusion, and hoping to dazzle her with my flawless memory for faces and names I said: "Harriet? Harriet Sinje?"

She smiled a kind, soft, and very sweet smile. Encouraging my advance, she said, "Thank you." But then she added, "I wish I looked like Harriet." My dismay must have been apparent. She continued, "A lot of people mistake me for Harriet, but I'm not her."

"You look exactly like her," I said, shock and incredulity still on my sleeve. "I went to public school with her."

"She's changed since then," said the redhead. "She's become a lot more beautiful. People stop me all the time and take me for her, but I only wish I looked like she does."

We chatted a bit about where Harriet lived now, far out on Long Island. That she was married. Her extraordinary looks. I thanked the woman. She walked off.

I never saw Harriet after that and I had not been to Douglaston for more than twenty years. Not that I was planning on it, but I did wonder, if I ever ventured out Queens way, what the odds would be of bumping into the real Harriet after so many years. After all, I had run into just about everyone else. More or less, mostly more I suppose, it may indeed have been statistically about time perhaps for just one sighting. Of course, my friend had advised against it. But he was wrong. And don't they say something about hope springing eternal? I hoped, on the one hand, that my luck would hold and I would never run into Harriet again.

On the other hand, I thought, maybe one of these days...
who knows? What would be the chances? The odds?

The Y

All the hotshot twelve-year-old boys ran around with their orange books, folded and dog-eared, protruding from the back pockets of their corduroy pants. They were on their way to manhood, soon to become thirteen; soon to be initiated into that sacred rite to which only the boys, men of tomorrow, were privy. There were few of the unsightly basic Hebrew primers, few of yesterday's scribbled upon notebooks in view. The creased-in-half, orange, haphtorah booklets minimally said all there was to say. Commencement was almost here, advancement was being pursued, the dust of childhood left behind. The more creased and soiled, the more ragged the booklet of readings, the higher the holder was on the heroic scale, the more senior on this short journey. For there were those fledglings who had just received their brand new books, whose orange covers were crisp and unbroken, as yet unbent back to reveal the secrets and challenges within.

The orange booklets, however, were not revealed in the public school and rarely flashed on the streets of Washington Heights. Their province was the YMWHA on 178th Street and Fort Washington Avenue, known to all as the Y, with its noble view westward of the George Washington Bridge. Their dominion was the classroom down the creaky wooden slatted hallway on the second floor, and the tile-floored recreation room at the Y's southernmost end on the first floor...where the ping-pong tables were.

Ping-pong at the Y, after public school was out, presided over by the dashing and sage Bert, the young attorney and role model who also reigned supreme over the game, was not the only attraction in the rec room. There were the femmes, three of whom come to mind. I can see them seated on the maroon built-in bench, ensconced in the little wall niche, the three of them: Ruby, Marcia, and Harriet. They were from another public school, probably P.S. 132. (This Harriet was a different Harriet from the inamorata of my imagination at P.S. 173, and different in every respect.) Marcia and Harriet were sweet, articulate, approachable, and a year or two older than most of the boys in the rec room. Marcia had wonderfully symmetrical features with a generous smile of dazzling white, even teeth, revealed by her readily parting full lips. She wore her dark brown hair in a frizzy afro, long before that style became popular. We were nearly a decade away from that. Harriet had a warm, round, and cheerful face, always a pleasant expression. And yet it was Ruby, quiet, withdrawn, Ruby who had the secret attentions and hearts of most of the young boys. It was the strawberry blonde Ruby with her high cheekbones and short hair, her closely-held smile and paucity with words that had us captivated. Marcia and Harriet were the mother confessors, the friends, the confidantes. Ruby was the reason, the allure. Ruby was the gem.

In Music and Art High School, in New York, as an entering freshman, I was surprised to find Marcia, already in her sophomore year. We became friends, although not close friends. She still had her ready smile and warmth. She was still older and a class ahead. Years later, when I saw her photo in someone's yearbook, I recalled her vividly and became acutely aware of the rare glow of her that I had foolishly overlooked. In 1956, as an entering student at Hunter College, I ran into Ruby in the cafeteria. She had changed. The peach in her face was gone. Enticement and intrigue had vaporized. A faint smile of recognition passed between us, some amenable words. I continued on with my lunch tray. She was another coed, lunching quietly, alone.

A fellow who made frequent visits to the ping-pong room was a feisty, freckle-faced character named Bob Rothstein, also a year or two my senior. Rothstein used to take off early on Fridays. He claimed to have a part-time job on the radio. I found it difficult to believe that he was actually on the radio. I was completely unfamiliar with small-town radio and had only known of, had only ever heard, New York's 50,000-watt stations, like WOR, WJZ, WHN, WCBS, NBC, WNYC, WNEW, and WQXR. You did not casually work at any of these. And certainly not if you had any kind of speech impediment. Rothstein stuttered. But he wasn't fabricating. He truly had a job broadcasting at some little thousand-watt daytimer out of town. Maybe he didn't stutter when he was on the air. But it was a revelation to me. He was an early hero.

When it was time for class, Robert Fried and I met at the candy stand on the first floor of the Y and purchased two-round pretzels. We broke them into smaller pieces which we placed in our shirt pockets and went upstairs. The idea was to sneak a piece of pretzel into your mouth without being seen, keep it in there for as long as possible without chewing it, and finally, make the pocketful last until the end of class. It was about an hour. It was a challenge. We rarely made it. But the triple task saw us through the class.

My friend Malcolm lived across the street from me. His home life, however, was as alien to mine as could be. Malcolm was not an only child, as I was. He had a brother, Arnold, who was many years older, sullen, angry, and in fact never smiled, certainly not in Malcolm's or my presence. The idea conveyed to the world by Arnold was that he wished nothing whatever to do with Malcolm. Malcolm seemed to convey that he did not like Arnold. And, indeed, Arnold did not seem a likeable person.

The only person in the household with whom Arnold may have had an amicable relationship was Toby, his sister, closest in age to him. Toby was an extremely good-looking girl, probably one of the best-looking young women I have ever seen. When I met Malcolm years later, one of the first things he said to me was, "Remember my sister Toby? She turned into a house."

Arnold's other sister was Rhoda, a nice-looking, sweet girl, best remembered by me for arbitrating disputes between Malcolm and everybody else. Rhoda was only a couple of years older than Malcolm, but I can recall her changing, approaching larger sizes, as her teen years rolled along.

Malcolm himself was a skinny kid, a result perhaps of his hyperactivity. He was extremely intelligent, well-read, but trouble. He never stood still, punctuated nearly all of his communications with punches, his somewhat angry disposition seamlessly transformed into nonstop mischief and teasing. And no visit to his apartment was anything less than chaotic, beyond indecipherable noise and screaming, verbal conflagrations, and hardly welcome-wagonish. Malcolm was a latecomer to his family and, I gathered, somewhat of a surprise. It was not a milk-and-cookies household.

There were books in Malcolm's life, but no toys that I can recall. And for his thirteenth birthday, I remember his mother taking our friend Ross, Malcolm, and myself to the local Cantonese Chinese restaurant on Broadway, where we had egg rolls, chow mein, spare ribs, and Cokes.

Sometime later, my thirteenth birthday arrived. Today, this milestone has become an extravaganza, the treatment having begun some years ago at the likes of Leonard's of Great Neck and going so far as celebrations being conducted at the Wailing Wall in Jerusalem, in an effort to outdo, if not keep up with, contest. My party was quite memorable, held in our two-room apartment with friends and neighbors spilling out into the hallway. My father had saved liquor, one bottle at a time, over the course of a year, until, by the time of the fete, he had a full complement to accommodate the guests of the gala. Meanwhile, I had performed the stuff in my little orange book pretty well. And I received much of what I had wanted in the way of gifts: a few wallets, and six portfolio-type briefcases that were in vogue at the time. The party could have been held on Noah's Ark. It couldn't have been better nor more memorable for me. I felt I had acquitted myself and my family. That was really enough.

One of the outstanding gifts I had received came from my father's office staff. It was a Voit basketball. I had never owned a basketball, and this one seemed quite legitimate and fairly expensive as basketballs go. My father knew nothing about basketballs, but was proud to present this one to me, equally gratified at the clever choice his office had made in selecting this quality boy's delight. It quickly was afforded favored status in my life, to the chagrin of downstairs neighbors, and was the first thing I dribbled on the hardwood floors when I came home from school and threw my books down. (We were some forty years from backpacks.)

It seemed to be an instant hit with my friends as well. I was now the only kid with a basketball. Not everyone had all the sports items necessary to get up a game. Someone had a football…**the** football; someone had the good bat, now I had the basketball. But it was not so much instant popularity as it was instant pestering. "Why don't you go up and get the basketball?" became the question of the day…every day.

One Saturday morning, only a week or so after I had it out of the box, I brought it downstairs. It wasn't as if we had real baskets or basketball courts; we shot from the sidewalks through fire escape rungs. We took set shots, jump shots, lay-ups and played consecutive games of one-on-one. We had a good time…for a couple of hours. And it was difficult to take the plaything away, to remove the very cement of our mutual fun, our Saturday, and go upstairs. So the entourage followed me into the entryway to 20 Cabrini Boulevard, flanked by hedges penned in by painted green wrought iron spikes. That's when Malcolm thought up the new, impromptu game.

The farewell, entryway game consisted simply of throwing the basketball over the hedges against the side wall. The next fellow was to catch it and throw it against the wall, to the third man. Of course, the throws became increasingly hard until the game turned into a hurling frenzy. The inevitable happened. On an especially vicious throw by Malcolm, at an unfortunate angle, the wall returned the basketball onto one of the iron spikes. I had never viewed them as sharp or harmful before, but in that one abrupt moment of perforation, hiss, and deflation, I felt stunned and shaken by a newly learned reality. The mildness of an almost invisible old friend showed itself to have another side. The benevolence of what had become a nearly unnoticed piece of the landscape over the years was no longer to be trusted and had, along with my basketball, been punctured. And so was my life at home for the next several months.

The three of us trekked to Broadway and down as far as 168th Street to try and get the thing patched and back to where it would be functional. But it was no good. We hiked from service station to auto body shop to gas station before somebody threw a meaningless patch on the ball. But it was cosmetic. The bladder was ruined and the ball was dead. I had hoped, at least, to be able to get it into the house unobtrusively, but that didn't work either. My sham was seen through just as the ball was pierced. I tried to call it an accident, but in the end I took the blame and the reproach that came with it. I was impugned as one who could not take care of his possessions, censured as careless and irresponsible. I did not deserve such a gift that I had just ruined, but was rebuked as reckless, ungrateful, and unworthy. I would never forget this, particularly as it was raised many times to reaffirm the lesson. I never owned another basketball.

The patched hole in the Voit basketball never healed, and neither did I from this incident. But some years later, it occurred to me as I recalled the "accident," I might better have focused not so much on my own carelessness as on the somewhat overzealous, if not malicious, throw of a boy whose material possessions were few and whose sole commemoration into manhood was a Chinese dinner.

CENTER ROW: "MALCOLM, ?, ROSS, ME, ALAN"

Sid Stone

Tuesday nights at 8 PM. If you did not have a television, one of those blurry, sometimes blue-screened, magnified jobs with the rabbit ears, whose picture was forever lapsing into vertical rolls and horizontal misalignment, you were generally invited next door, upstairs or downstairs to view the *Texaco Star Theater* starring Milton Berle. Uncle Miltie. My hero, however, was not Berle. It was the Texaco pitchman who appeared sometime around mid-show for the commercial break. A guy named Sid Stone.

He stood alone on the stage behind his box of wares, mostly Texaco products, which was perched on a folding stand, and he wore a checked sport jacket and bowler hat. He pulled his shirt sleeves up and over his jacket sleeves and energetically launched into his carnie-like spiel, selling Texaco Havoline Motor Oil, Super Chief, Fire Chief, and related products, invariably leading to his signature phrase: "You say you're not sat-is-fi-yed... you say you want more for your money? Step right up here...I'll tell you what I'm gonna do." The bit usually ended with a whistle being blown off stage, signaling the arrival of the police. Stone would yell "Cops!" fold up his stand, and take off in a run.

Sid Stone, the tall, dark, and good-looking pitchman, was always an amusing favorite but he became a superstar to me when I learned he resided on Pinehurst Avenue in Washington Heights, only one short block from Cabrini Boulevard, where I lived. I had only seen him in the neighborhood once, without the checked jacket and bowler hat and was surprised at his striking appearance and how tall he was, well over six feet. I would have guessed six-feet-four.

Someone in our building had a connection to Texaco, NBC, Stone himself, or his wife Celia, and I wound up with a genuine Sid Stone Junior Pitchman Kit. It was complete with wooden stand, cardboard box of stuff, and paper bowler hat. In short order, I mastered the barker's inflection and nasal twang, and, in fact, I actually sounded like him. Soon I had the nerve to perform Sid Stone impressions at Miss Duffy's class parties during the entertainment segment, and although I had only seen him once or twice in our neighborhood, I told people I knew him.

As the *Texaco Star Theater* gained in popularity, so did Sid Stone. He became a favorite on the show to such an extent that, from what we neighbors understood from his wife and one of his daughters, he rivaled Milton Berle. Word was, contrary to what fans would surmise from the two comics' public personas, they did not get along, and production meetings were heated. Stone's wife said Berle was jealous of Sid, things were getting worse, and despite his popularity and apparent success, Stone was not happy. The two men irreparably disliked one another.

The pitchman continued on the show for a while, but his segments, it seemed, grew shorter and more infrequent. I remember seeing more of the four singing Texaco gas jockeys: "Oh we're the men of Texaco...We work from Maine to Mexico...There's nothing like this Texaco of ours...." There was less of Sid Stone.

Sometime in the early fifties, we learned a tragic automobile accident took the life of one of Stone's two daughters. By then, the Berle show had diminished in popularity and little was heard of Sid Stone.

I was a junior in high school a couple of years later, and one of my classmates got the bright idea of playing hooky so we could take the Union City, New Jersey bus across the G.W. Bridge to the Hudson Burlesque House... for the matinee. I remember him saying it was the jokes... the comedians. "Wait 'til you hear the jokes." We did stay out of school that day and headed for Union City, one of the area's last burlesque holdouts. The bus ride, carrying twenty to thirty middle-aged men, was not especially long, but no one got off at any of the stops. When finally the bus reached the Hudson Theater, the driver announced: "Last stop, Metropolitan Opera." Everyone chuckled. Everyone got off.

The show wasn't bad. The comedians weren't that funny, and when the girls stripped, the drummer, one of a trio of musicians, played the same beat. It was embarrassing. As my friend and I were about to leave, a pitchman appeared in one of the aisles and began shouting over the din, selling some kind of confection in a red and white box. He held up the cardboard container and said, if the crunchy-munchy candy wasn't delicious enough, you could hold the box up to the light and see the hidden dancing girl do all kinds of shimmying tricks. For only fifty cents. Four bits. Two thin quarters! It was Sid Stone, wearing a white smock and white ducks…like the ice-cream man. No bowler. No checked jacket. He didn't look too tired and somehow was able to muster the incredible energy and vocal force that was his trademark… that was necessary for the afternoon. But few seemed to notice. The show was over. "You say you're not satis-fi-yed, you say you want more for your money? Step right up here…I'll tell you what I'm gonna do!"

WINTER

Zeppelin Man

For some time lately, I have been taken with the notion of blimps. Zeppelins, dirigibles, blimps. I watch for them, note their appearance overhead, seek out their likeness, and collect them. I have collected photos, models, miniatures, magazine articles, books, toys, accessories, badges, buttons, and blow-ups...inflatables. I wasn't sure what lay behind the compulsion, what the compelling impetus was, but I derived something pleasant and perhaps even necessary each time I acquired anything...blimpish. It brought to mind a vague recollection, well buried, out of consciousness. One day I received a pamphlet I had won in an auction. I had never seen anything like it. It was a public relations brochure for Good Year hyping the company's "Aerial Ambassadors." The entire booklet was dedicated to the Good Year blimps. The gentleman from whom I obtained this little gem confessed to having kept it for the last several years because of a fascination he had as a boy in the 1950s watching the blimps take off and land near where he lived in Florida, before he moved to the Bronx, N.Y. We chatted and found we shared many experiences during that period.

When I received the piece, I found it to have been carefully wrapped and packaged with plastics and envelopes. The pamphlet itself was well preserved, for a paper item over thirty years old, picturing three Good Year blimps and a couple of hundred balloons on the blue cover. Inside, the illustrations were also blue, some of the borders silvery gray. I didn't expect that much in the way of revelation when I perused the piece, but I was overtaken by nostalgic reverie.

Some years ago, during a lecture on broadcast communications to a college class I was attempting to teach, I found myself waxing dramatic over the reasons why the *Hindenburg* debacle was considered such a catastrophe through the years, in light of the fact that there have been so many equally disastrous and more costly losses. I speculated that the event came on the heels of the Great Depression, at a time when few, if any, could afford to travel anywhere. It came when few had ever flown and could only dream about that great adventure in the air, floating high above earthly concerns. They imagined themselves not only floating joyously through the ecstasy-inducing ether, but living the high life figuratively as well, dancing through the skies, dining on delicacies, immaculately clad, laughing, drinking champagne, on their cheerful ways to and from wonderful places. So, glancing skyward at this remarkable vessel, the size of a football field, so high above the gray street and the dim homes and the grim, colorless, hard lives, the ground people saw hope. They invested themselves, along with their hopes, in dreams of travel, destiny, wonder and enchantment, excellent foods, music and fine things, festivity and love. And, for a few moments, they were there. They were up in the sky with the splendor and the beauty, the things that might be. And then…there was no more "might be." What did materialize was conflagration of hope and blasted dreams; the cruelest disappointment, so undeniably real for all to see. That which offered at least the hope, the momentary fantasy, was irreparably torn, burnt, and destroyed; and with it those light and airy thoughts and excursions of wonder for millions. That was why, I offered, the *Hindenburg* disaster was so devastating, more so than the countless tragedies before or since. But as I glanced through the blimp pamphlet years later, I recalled yet another incident perhaps pertinent to my collecting obsession.

On a cold November morning, my parents took me to the New York Macy's Thanksgiving Day parade. It was extremely frosty and we found a place to view the parade deep in the crowd lined against the western wall of Central Park. From my father's shoulders, I could see a man across the street, a street vendor, selling blown-up Good Year blimps on a wooden stick. I can still recall the price. It was fifty cents. Back in the 1940s, this was a considerable sum for a street-bought toy. But, I can almost feel the intense and burning desire I had for this item. I had never seen anything like it. It was so big, seriously shaped, and seriously gray. It seemed to possess the capacity to lift you up…and up. Surely it could do something like that. It was filled with real helium and the envelope could have been of who-knew-what-kind of wonderful material. I not only wanted…I needed this thing. Zeppelin, the man called it…helium-filled zeppelin. The hordes, though, would not allow passage from one side of the street to the other, and besides, fifty cents seemed prohibitive. My parents assured me, however, that after the parade, they would make the purchase. It was then all I could think of that morning. I would have my Zeppelin. The parade passed. The man and his helium-filled zeppelins vanished and were not to be found. We looked down several streets. Gone.

Now, in the midst of everyday life, friends around me are falling ill and many are caught up in downward spirals. Time seems to be thrusting us on our way along a steep slope with its disconcerting peripheral vistas of life's detritus strewn about. One feels the angst at knowing, or at the very least fearing, that we too, are soon to become just so much flotsam and jetsam.

I look at the Good Year booklet with its serene sky blue cover and its tranquilizing one-color photos inside, and I think of my students with benumbed expressions on their faces, completely incapable of understanding the enormity of the *Hindenburg* disaster.

I recall the man who sent me the pamphlet, and how he stood at his vantage point down south, so many years ago, watching the launchings and landings of the great airships of wonder, and how he carefully wrapped and sealed this magical packet of the past, and I begin to know why I pursue these lofty air-filled things, these dreams. And I remember, too, how the man with the helium-filled blimps, the zeppelins, vanished forever.

The Return

In my pocket I have a Saint Gaudens twenty-dollar gold piece with the date worn to obscurity. For some, this will assuredly not suffice as any kind of proof of this story, although perhaps inherent reason and logic will furnish adequate confirmation of what took place.

The house could have been any Washington Heights apartment building. But to me, it was mine; where I had always lived. The color of its brick was off-white. It stood on the corner of 178th Street and Cabrini Boulevard on the Upper West Side of Manhattan, across the street from the immense George Washington Bridge, which spanned the Hudson to Fort Lee, New Jersey.

On hot summer evenings, we would bring folding chairs downstairs to the corner and sit up late into the night with neighbors, enjoying the breeze from the river, keeping cool.

Old Mr. Collins, who had been building superintendent at one time, was almost always there. A big man, and former U.S. Marine who had fought in the Spanish-American War, he was a retired mounted policeman and one-time keeper of the small red lighthouse situated on the rocks of the Hudson beneath the bridge. Mr. Collins was the nucleus of the group, and I felt a special importance because he lived on our floor, around the bend in apartment 4A.

Mrs. Berman, from upstairs on the fifth floor, was almost always in attendance as well. She was getting very old and quiet, and I cannot recall anything to characterize her beyond: Mrs. Berman, fifth floor, upstairs.

There were also the Millers and the Schweds, ground floor neighbors who were best friends and whose children enjoyed the additional convenience of receiving ice-cream money or jackets through windows without having to go inside.

Others passed by and stopped to talk but were by no means regulars. They were only, not unfamiliar faces. They were neighbors who never sat down, outside on the corner, with us those hot summer nights.

I had spent many a summer vacation away. How odd the six-story house seemed when I returned. It was not strange, because it was so familiar. It was not different. It had not changed at all. It was odd, because I had changed and it had not. It occurred to me that I had moved, been away and grown while the house had not. It was, during those late, hot, dry summer days, as always, tall and quiet, on the corner, off-white. Each window was familiar, as was each pavement crack, and scratched and painted initials on the bricks, chinks, and notched crevices in the cement between.

They were all still there, as I had left them. Nothing had changed. Yet.

In time, a long expressway would be built; some blocks east, a bus terminal. And the house on Cabrini Boulevard was razed. Only memories were left of its cool image in the early evening blue, waiting as we came back from Broadway, the taste of a chocolate soda still on our lips. Hours later, its early-morning smile would reflect the sun's glare. But now its familiar, informal reign on the windy corner for twenty-five years was over.

I had been away and alone, and had on occasion been obsessed with thoughts of the old neighborhood, particularly the house. I pictured the corner, the street and the sidewalk in front of the building. During one of these mental excursions, I focused on an almost forgotten detail.

In front of the apartment house, built into the sidewalk, was a black, iron trap door. It opened on a coal chute to the cellar, and was used exclusively for the delivery of coal. The major difference between this and other neighborhood coal chutes was that it was on the sidewalk, not vertically built into the side of the building. It was smaller than the iron doors found on street freight elevators, and could be opened with a single finger or crowbar inserted into a hole across from the hinge. The door was about two feet square.

Shortly after the new expressway was completed, I had been back to the old street and found in place of our house, a pleasant bit of park, raised and set back several feet. Around and above the little park area ran the expressway. Otherwise, except for a breezy emptiness, everything was the same. I had not noticed anything more.

I came to wonder if they hadn't done away with the iron door. Most likely they had, although I did not recall any apparent change in the pavement, and why alter the street, since the little park was built a considerable distance back from it? It was then I became preoccupied with thoughts of the coal chute and thought, if it was still there, where did it now lead? I had seen where many times as a child.

It was on a vacant day in September, I decided, out of a peculiar mixture of nostalgia and curiosity, to revisit the site of my old beloved house. It was a long walk from the Fort Washington Avenue bus stop, made even longer by the emptiness in the streets, the lack of familiar faces; the bowing warp of time. The walls of the buildings still standing, the familiar landmarks, seemed mute with the shyness of a child who has not seen a friend in a long time. The warmth in the air waited to be shook by the shrill call of one boy to another or the whipping swing of a stickball bat putting a pink ball high on a flowerpotted fire escape, or the song of the huckster selling fruit, cashing clothes, or sharpening knives.

Looking up, I could see the apartment where Ross used to live. Behind it, I thought I saw Ross and his mother and father, his big brother Irv, and myself, sitting in the living room, waiting to go downstairs. On my left was Bernie's window. There was no shade, no curtain hanging. I knocked. It was dusty and black on the inside. I waited. No one came.

The house was only a half block away. On the corner was Biderman's Grocery Store. I could see it was closed, but I quickened my pace, nearly breaking into a jog, because in Biderman's, you could get salami on a hard roll, ice cold

Doc's Root Beer, and fresh chocolate- or vanilla-frosted cupcakes from the box. Jack the postman was often inside eating lunch, sitting on the one wooden and wrought iron stool that stood forever before Biderman's marble-topped counter. Lenny the salesman, stopping in on his way home, would tell a funny story while buying groceries, and Harry, Biderman's assistant, pencil behind his ear, leaning on the countertop was, on slow afternoons, good for a coin trick, catching flies, or moving his ears. To his left were neatly placed boxes of Joyva Halvah, chocolate-covered jellies, and marshmallow twists for two cents apiece. I stood before the mini-flight of three concrete steps leaning into the store. Years ago, when Biderman's was in its heyday, and nearly everyone in the neighborhood shopped there to some degree, I overheard someone say it was a goldmine. Since Biderman's son didn't want any part of the place and Biderman was aging, some people jealously remarked about Harry's good fortune as heir apparent to the place. After all, he wasn't even a relation; just a hired young man. Now, some hardware and a couple of pairs of workman's gloves hung on the door window.

Across the street were the park, the emptiness and—not seeming strange at all, just where it had always been—the iron door. I stopped in front of it, and through the rainbow emanating from the park, paused to dream of slug, bike rides, scooters, and skates, and the grinding racket their wheels made on the concrete sidewalk. And I could envision a little boy standing on that very spot. For a moment, I thought of going home, but the notion gave way to scanning the area. Was I being observed? It was then I reached down, as if to tie my shoelace, and inserted a finger through the hole opposite the rusting hinge. The door was heavy but opened easily, as if it were not I who was lifting it but the winds of the past blowing it open for me.

The opening disclosed a gaping blackness. Of course, I expected nothing more. Sitting on the edge, my legs dangling in the hole, I took hold of one side and swung down into the pit, none too deftly, landing on a heap of coal. The shock of falling made me stop moving for a moment. Time itself seemed to have come to an abrupt halt. Then, as I attempted to step down, the coal gave way and I fell backward. Objects in the room began to swirl gently as they came into focus and took strange shapes. It was as if time and space were moving together, backward and away. It was not unlike eyes getting used to the dark.

When I got to my feet and stumbled down off the coal heap, I could make out the room. The contour of its dimensions was vividly familiar. It was the last of a chain of rooms and storage closets in the cellar of the old house. Were the others still intact as well? I could make out a door ahead. Certainly, I reasoned, the door led somewhere. It was splintered, dusty, and forbidding, but it had another side. As I reached for it, I realized the knob was gone but I managed to get the door open, like the sidewalk door, with a finger. One room led to the next. And not unexpectedly, they were all there: the carriage room, the boiler room, the storage room, the laundry room, the workshop, the incinerator, and then, finally, incredibly, the elevator.

A rush of memories returned to me: Willie the handyman taking what seemed like weeks to paint my little red car white; Henry the elevator man bringing the car up to the apartment, where I then quickly outgrew it and it was relegated to becoming a receptacle for newspapers and magazines. I saw myself watching the final cycle of a washing machine, helping my mother hang clothes, and years later, exploring the dark basement labyrinths with a friend after school... with the aid of matchbooks. The explorations had become less exciting when we began using what we thought would be the more efficient candles. Nothing could equal the pressure and urgency, the chill of the blackness and nebulous danger when the match burned down and out. And nothing was as inevitable as the brief lifespan of the paper match, hardly equal to the two elements in our explorations that always loomed before us. Always presenting hidden danger, always possibilities that could frighten us to death, always lurking were: the superintendent...and the dog. We bravely stood ready to deal with them, but our progress—that is, the high-tech move to candles, and later to flashlights—not only lessened the surprise of these dangers and softened the challenges of our underground explorations, they dampened the entire experience, and soon put an end to them as well.

As I rang for the elevator, I watched the red arrow, which pointed down, begin to glow. Through the round glass window in the door, I could see the cables move and faintly was able to hear a hum from within the elevator shaft. Other than that persistent sound, everything remained probably as still as it had been for the past two decades. I had to wonder where the elevator was coming from. I knew there was no house. The building had been taken down years ago. Yet I was following what seemed to be a logical sequence of events. Was this making sense? The hum stopped and the inner elevator door opened.

I pulled at the outer door, and stepping in, recognized the peculiar designs on the walls. There were old scratched and worn black buttons. Everything was exactly as I recalled and the words, "coincidence," "nightmare," and "hallucination" came to mind. I wiped perspiration from my face, my legs felt weak and shaky; my body began to shiver involuntarily. And already, without being aware of it, the thought had crossed my mind, terrifying me. There was one supreme test, one inevitability, one place to go. With some reservation, yet still determined, I pressed the fourth floor button.

As I ascended, the light which came through the little chicken wire round hole became brighter with each floor. The car came to a stop at four, the inner door opened, and I pushed at the heavier door to step off.

Across from the elevator was a large hall window. Outside, below, was the courtyard littered with glass, paper, and small planks of wood. It was a treasure trove for young pirates, who would—despite informal prohibitions—be sure to climb daily through the ground floor access windows to sift through the debris. Sun suffused the six stories above the yard, shining on the refuse with gleams, increasing its apparent value to the impish hunters a thousand fold.

I crossed the floor parallel with the stairwell to the first apartment on the left of the elevator, 4E, my old apartment. For a moment, I stood before it. Everything was, or seemed, as it had always been: the brown door flecked with gold paint, the fading welcome mat, the protruding bell, the only one on the floor which had not been painted over, our name beneath it. I distracted myself with thoughts of the Collinses around the bend in 4A, the Millers downstairs, and Mrs. Berman above, on 5. So far, however, I reminded myself, I had not seen a soul. Numb, I stood transfixed. Then I pressed the bell. I remembered the ring.

"Who is it?" a small but pleasant-sounding voice asked from behind the door. I hesitated.

"A…visitor," I replied. And at once, I had a startling recollection. I had experienced a similar incident when I was a boy. Someone had rung the bell and when I inquired as to who it was, the voice responded with, "A visitor." Although I had repeatedly been instructed never to open the door to strangers, I recall having had a contrary compulsion to do so. It was almost as if I had known my own father was there. The door opened wide.

Speech seemed to catch in my throat.

"Hello," I managed. The boy was me as a child, about eight or nine years old. I couldn't take my eyes from him. I wanted to grab him up and take him with me, show him everything I knew, and teach him a thousand things. I felt compelled to give him countless warnings. I wanted to bestow on him all my possessions. Beyond the boy, I could see past his yellow slip-over sweater, through the little foyer, and into the living room along the furniture I knew so well. Each piece was in its proper place. I wanted to touch every article; sit at the table; turn on the lamp; feel the chairs again. Instead, I could only stand, immobile, in my place.

"My mother isn't home," the little boy said, his eyes clear and blue. For an instant, I saw myself staring out into an adult world of truths and perplexities, however modified by my own childish concepts and feelings. I had the feeling of understanding him completely.

"Well…" I said softly, "it doesn't really matter. I have something I want to give to you."

In my pocket, I always carried a gold coin which was given to me when I was a young boy by the stranger whom I found standing at my door that afternoon. He had paid his visit for no other apparent reason. I remember being struck by the word "Liberty" engraved on the coin…and its being solid gold.

"Keep this and don't lose it," I said. "And don't let anyone take it away from you." He took it and fondled it.

"Thanks," he drew out as he admired it. "Can I really keep it?"

"It's yours," I said. "Perhaps I'll see you again."

Then I left. The elevator was waiting. I pressed "B" and took it to the basement; I ran through the cellar rooms to the coal bin, climbed through the iron door and pulled myself up into the street. On my way to the Fort Washington Avenue bus stop, I turned around but once, only to see the blowing leaves in the park on Cabrini Boulevard.

Some years had passed. The memory of the coin faded, almost as if I never really owned it. The trip to Cabrini Boulevard could have been a dream. I never went back. The days were fraught with depression and loneliness, at times, an empty coolness draining warmth and life from the body.

It was at the end of a day, on an evening particularly laden with chill, that I answered a knock at my door. I had, for sometime now, been residing in another city, far away, and kept to myself. So when the elderly gentleman at the door, whom I had never set eyes upon before, addressed me by my first name, it was not without surprise.

"I think," he said, "you must know who I am. Or you will." A kindly smile pushed his age aside.

"I'm sorry. I don't believe I do," I replied. "Can I help you?" The old man kept his eyes focused on me as he spoke but seemed to take the opportunity of my reply to peer beyond me and into the apartment.

"I used to live here myself," he paused. "I find myself missing those days quite a bit now."

Smiling, I said, "You couldn't have lived here, this building is brand new."

"Is it?" said the old man. I suddenly realized who he was. He knew I had and he grinned again.

"How is it there?" I gulped out, hardly able to manage clear speech.

"It's the same," he said, "a little lonely."

I was seized with an energy I could not contain. Questions I could not frame as I sensed a certain urgency about him. "Could I go back with you?" He looked about with venerable eyes and said:

"Yes…and no."

"What do you mean?" I asked, my heart pounding.

"You cannot go back with me," he said, "but you will go there. Alone."

There was very little light left in the hallway. It had all drained away through cracks and nooks, doors and windows. The old man stood on his side of the threshold in his overcoat, I, on my side, in my shirtsleeves. Behind me, the apartment, darkening, gaping, empty. He put his hand into a deep pocket.

"Incidentally," he said, "I came back here to return this to you. I believe you left it somewhere along the way." He held out the gold piece. It was the St. Gaudens with the date worn away.

"Where did you get it?" I asked.

"An old man gave it to me nearly thirty-five years ago. You know it's yours."

I looked at the coin's face. The word "Liberty" on it had hardly worn. It was exactly as I had remembered it.

"Keep it and don't lose it," the old man cautioned. He grinned, took a last look beyond me, and then disappeared across the hall.

"Will I see you again?" I called after him. He didn't answer. "I'll see you again," I muttered under my breath. But he was gone. Fingering the coin, I stepped back into the apartment and closed the door.

Through the open window, I could discern the orange image of the faceless sun floating above everything. The air was still but once in a while, some refreshing breeze filled the room.

178ᵗʰ STREET AND CABRINI BLVD. BY GWB

"MR. COLLINS, ME, MOM"

The Last Stand

On the corner of 178th Street and Fort Washington Avenue, diagonally across the street from the old YMWHA, on whose site is now the Port Authority Bus Terminal, there was a wooden, olive drab newsstand. In the evening, you could pick up a late paper or perhaps a copy of *The Saturday Evening Post* before hopping aboard the downtown number four, Fifth Avenue bus. The newsy who carried just about everything inside the little hovel was a one-armed World War I vet who rarely spoke, but who knew all his customers, as they knew him, and who warmed the night corner with the flickering yellow light that glowed inside his booth. He sat quietly, some nights in a thirties newsy's cap, sometimes in his wool seaman's cap and ragged pea coat, as he awaited his last few customers for the late edition papers. In his heart, he had long tired of the same faces, people coming and going, while he sat and watched, and waited, and dreamed. It seemed as if he had long tired of the repeated amenities; the token exchanges. He never smiled.

Well beyond the visor of the frayed tweed cap he wore on this night, the old eyes in his craggy face turned toward the black sky and the stars afar, deep into so many nights. He might have created alien craft soaring out from the heavens, settling some distance before his earthly establishment to dispatch a dashing, or otherwise, spaceman toward him. And as the chilly winds blew along the George Washington Bridge from the rolling Hudson beneath it, certainly, he may have mused, the stranger and his companions, if there were any, should be drawn by his light, and should like to read of all the Earthly news. To the spaceman he would casually say, unruffled: "Paper, mister?"

But there was no ship. No spaceman; frequently no customers at all at this hour. Not yet.

***

He had journeyed, or so the records indicated, through the black vastness, the deep and empty reaches of space. Such a void of depth and emptiness did he traverse, that he had only to sleep through it; a sleep as deep, empty and black as those forever night realms through which he passed unknowingly. The hulking, silvery ship had carried him millions upon millions of miles through bleak and blurry light years from home to….

Now the rays of a warm sun, a different sun, beat down on the ship's multi-layered windows as the polyplex alloy shades lifted, filling the hulk's inner chambers with real light. And as his waking moments took shape in the swaddling of his cryochamber, it seemed like a fresh Saturday morning. But it was not.

He had last been awake some months earlier. It was a Thursday, then. It seemed like only hours ago, but checking the readout on the ship's computer, the M330, he found it to be sixteen weeks.

He rose, washed, exercised, and dressed. Then he ate. Checking further readouts on the M330, he flicked from line to bar graph, from color spectrum to texture, temperature and density scans. All the sequences were congruent. It was somewhat of a comfort. All seemed to be as expected.

Winston and Effington might have been pleased that, so far, all was going according to program. He felt the vacuum of their absence; the fear of being alone, but he had already dealt with the nightmare of his crewmembers' early and untimely demise months…years ago, when the accident occurred. He accessed their factor input charts and watched the printout of the substitution program he had affected with mission control when they were still reachable. The variables of Winston and Effington had been modified accordingly and the necessary accommodation made. Control had wiped the slate and rewritten the mission in mid-flight. Winston and Effington had never existed. But, he thought as he peered out the gaping polyplex window into the pulsing dark violet glow of the new sun, they had.

For four days and four nights in the new time, he orbited the pink sun's world making preparations for the ship's touchdown. He worked, watched, and dreamed as he shouldered his triple load. He pondered the ship, himself, the mission, and what awaited below.

The vessel had been through all of it. He had not. But, he thought with some guilt, he had survived. There was a certain pride in that. Now, however, the success of the mission's completion—and it was a considerable task—would be up to him…alone. He had a momentary heady sensation as he contemplated the changeover from automatic pilot to manual shifting. There was no one else to fall back on.

The constant and unbroken cloud cover, whose chemical composition was still in the process of being analyzed by M330, was growing into a source of depression. It gnawed at the thin shell of patience which still managed to contain his curiosity. From time to time, M330 showed enough latitude in conditions for him to drop altitude, which he did, but to little avail. The upper reaches of this stratosphere, with its heavy haze, seemed boundless, despite the computer's indications to the contrary. The ship nonetheless continued its easy spiral descent, quietly, until he noticed the change in the darkening purple pulsing outside.

He was not sure as to its cause, but M330 revealed the answer on its summary screen. First, each of its line and bar readouts showed a glitch where one should not have been. The aberration was apparent alongside its twin comparison trip program model. With each subsequent readout revealed by the wipe, the irregularity widened. Then the computer began showing variants of the glitch elsewhere along the lines and bars. These seemed to correspond to the pulsing outside.

On one of M330's sub screens a troubleshooting program operated on a one-step-ahead, factor-isolation principle. On it, a color depiction of the planet's rising sun loomed impressively. At its near quadrant on the face of the star, there was a tiny fleck. He might have overlooked the spot had it not been blinking like a cursor. He considered manually expediting the ship's spiral descent when the unexpected impact occurred. It jarred him, but was more like an electrostatic charge going through the entire ship. When he regained his senses and stood up, to the relief and realization that he was still alive, he noticed that ensuing readouts on M330 failed to make complete sense. One, however, did. One of the ship's reverse thrusters was knocked askew by the shock, and without them, a safe touchdown would not be possible. He saw too, one of the stabilizing gyros was thrown off and the ship was now losing altitude at an alarming rate. Further, there appeared to be a terrible turbulence outside. If he could realign the thrusters and at least modify the gyro problem, he might have a chance. But it would take time; at least an Earth hour or two. Fortunately the atmosphere of the huge planet below was that deep: a minimum, according to M330's charts, of three to four thousand miles from where he might be now.

With no little difficulty, jostled and bounced, he worked his way aft to reach what needed getting at. At one point, between adjustments which ended in the ship's listing, he noticed her cutting through the haze of strange clouds. The magenta pulsing was gone. The blackness was becoming sharp and clear. There was nothing visible out there now; not even a blurry fog by which he could gauge his movement. It looked as if he were not moving at all. But miles below, he knew, off to his right, was a white ball; quiet and slightly phosphorescent.

Outside the ship was a stillness that enveloped her; permeated her. He had arrived, coming in. He wondered to what. As the time passed, the ball grew larger; its phosphorescence diminishing; another layer of cloud cover becoming apparent. He thought his silver ship gliding in over the planet must look majestic, impressive, but wondered:

to whom? There were moments of expectation. There were flashes of…something more than just haze, night and barren landscape, but they were only flashes, no more than that.

Combining as much precision with haste as he possibly could, he replaced one of the damaged thruster's parts and the affected gyro was realigned. M330, however, was responding only partially, half-wittedly. He had no time to delve into its circuitry. But he ran a final readout, all of which seemed plausible, and assumed the controls. It was the last stage of the descent with touchdown quickly approaching.

His orbit had just eased him around to the night side of the planet and the big star was setting rapidly. This was not on the program. Margin of error was not half the planet. But it was too late for a correction. He was too low and his spiraling approach and rate of descent could not accommodate it. The thrusters were activated and he felt the ship list. Suddenly there was a wave of nausea and as it continued it was punctuated by periodic perspiration. He had the thought that the prospect of death, no matter where in the universe one happened to be, carried with it the same terrifying anguish. Then he began to ponder, once again, Control's mission.

A relatively nearby galaxy and each of several solar systems within it were selected on the basis of proximity, accessibility, and promise. That is to say, was there at least a probability the mission might bear fruit? The planet below him now was not known to bear life, but could sustain life. M330 and crew would reach it, explore it, mark it, seed it, and if possible, retrieve at least one of the long-dormant satellites and probes we dispatched. The usual quota of soil, rock, vegetation, and liquid samples would be expropriated;

experiments conducted on site; logs kept; transmitters erected; cameras set in place; monuments raised and a systematic search for life conducted.

But now, somehow, the mission seemed absurd to contemplate seriously. Survival and the question of what follows that were higher on his priority list of considerations. There would be plenty of time to execute Control's laundry list once he safely set foot down on…whatever it was down there.

Down there. It was a good deal closer now. It had, in fact, as its terrain filled M330's entire major viewing screen, by its growing proximity, transformed itself into reality. Soon, if he lived, he would be enmeshed in that reality, confident that it would be a reality not altogether dichotomous with his own. It would simply be an extension of his own reality. And yet, staring into the holographic viewing screen, it occurred to him that what he saw and was about to encounter was not so strikingly alien to him and could have existed anywhere. And this was, in fact, anywhere. It was just about as far "anywhere" as anyone so far as he knew had ever gone. For moments, he attempted to grasp, in his terms, just how far. He did not dwell on it. It was relative, wasn't it? The illusion, if not the reality, remained: It did not seem far. It could be…home.

The thruster had been firing for some time. A warning sound and the unmistakable voice of ailing M330 directed him to strap in and prepare for the final phase of braking and the last series of spirals before touchdown.

It was night. Purple night and he seemed to be gliding deeper into it as occasional patches of light came to him and faded. Still it remained clear. For interminable stretches, the terrain was unchanged, and unwavering night was bathed in unspoiled clarity. He maneuvered, corrected, and remaneuvered. Then, unexpectedly, the ship slowed on its own and helplessly banked as it had hours before in the pulsing. As if in a Herculean attempt to correct itself, it shocked the heavy stillness with an ear-splitting report, sounding as if her giant hull had cracked. She did not right herself, jolted, and then slammed into the planet's brush and soil, askew.

When at last he was able to pry open the hatch of his dying ship, he paused to marvel that he was alive. Then he looked deeply, reflectively and with awe into what surrounded him. The hulking ship had somehow fallen onto an elevated embankment from which he thought he could make out yards of relatively flat terrain, long clumps and stretches of brush and more flatland. Far off to his left, low cliffs formed a valley with this land on which he now stood, and configured a jagged outline of what seemed like ebony totems against the foreign sky. The steep and forbidding walls draped the scene menacingly but the fresh air was so still and the pitch so quiet as not to presage anything, good or evil.

He waited for morning, but it did not come. Perhaps he had slept through it. He couldn't be sure as M330 was no longer providing reliable indications of anything. Going through the ship, he laid out the standard lines of equipment which would enable the first of several excursions he was planning. At least his rover cart was working.

Not planning a lengthy exploration at first, he packed the buggy with a few essentials, lowered it from the ship and stood beside it, once again surveying this undisturbed indigo whose domain he was about to invade. It was then he saw it. He blinked his eyes. Far down into the valley, and then up, atop one of the flanking slopes there was a flicker, steady and distinct, like a beacon. It was the singular feature at the apparent terminus of the long landscape to draw and captivate his attention. He got into the RC1 and headed toward the light.

Most of the light that served to illuminate the terrain before him came from several moderately-sized moons. Together, though, they did not reflect as much light as Earth's one satellite; nor did there seem to be as many stars overhead as on a clear Earth night.

The RC1 buggy bounced and jiggled but tugged its load without too much strain. At times, it seemed to glide through hardly any ground resistance as it dashed toward the light. But the glowing light did not change in size or brightness. It did not appear to be getting any closer.

It was more than a night's ride; he wanted to rest, but he would not allow himself to, and he would not turn back. It was still black night and the valley was endless. From time to time, long patches of thicket would fall between his line of sight and the beacon, but always, as the buggy sped through to the clearing that lay ahead, the yellowish flicker reappeared, undisturbed.

Occasionally he dozed, momentarily consumed with fatigue, only to be jarred awake by a bounce, snapped into a quick consciousness parallel with a panicky scan of the horizon. He knew he had slept, not so much by his abrupt awakenings, but by the dream imagery his mind had begun to form during these mini-naps. At first, no more than converging lines and quilty patches formed his images, but as his exhaustion increased, the lines took on more intricate shapes and the patches dissolved into speedy, senseless mini-plots. One such plot saw several suns rising at various points along the planet's horizons, creating an enormous convergence of shadow which, when combined with the sunlight, blocked out both the beacon and its site...and it was lost to him.

Another dream had him traveling away from an ever-receding light source only to discover it being a faint star on the horizon. The dreams continued until the dark, flanking slopes gradually leveled out and, to his astonishment, he found himself on an equal plane with the amber twinkle. It was only then he rested and had something to eat.

The RC1 had plenty of muon fuel and seemed in fine shape. Still, there was a substantial area of thicket ahead, and while taking a short exploratory on foot, mostly for exercise, he opted to go the distance that way now that he could clearly make out the glimmer through the bramble. And perhaps walking might change his luck.

He was quite unaware of the passage of time, more so of distance. Only once, and only for an instant, did he give thought to the ship, envisioning it much farther down the plain than it was in actuality. But with ship and cart behind, quite alone now, he began to stumble.

The beacon was now beginning to come into focus through the brush, as the low star grouping on the horizon, of which his yellow gleam might have been a member, became obscured. He ran through the tangle of thorny vegetation that cut and pierced his suit and scratched his steamy visor until he removed it. A solitary figure in this alien planet night, he stumbled and pulled himself forward, tearing through the undergrowth of this remote sphere, this forlorn point in nowhere, everywhere, anywhere.

The dark green wood thinned and parted and cast out its visitor. It was almost within reach, he thought, as he looked up. And then some three hundred yards down, for the first time, he thought he could see it clearly. It stood alone: a beat-up, painted-over, olive drab, wooden, dimly-lit newsstand. Inside, under a slightly flickering yellow light, half-hidden behind a stack of freshly-printed newspapers was a wizened, tweed-capped newsy. From beneath a backdrop of sweets and crisply-colored magazines, the newsy, no smile on his craggy face, drew out a late paper. The hardly-discernable breeze that it fanned forth bore the scent of ink. The old man held it out. "Paper, mister?" he said.

He groped for change in his suit, bought a late Edition Journal American, Herald Tribune, Daily Mirror, World Telegram & Sun, Daily News, New York Times and New York Post; a couple of pulp magazines, *Collier's* and the *Saturday Evening Post*. He bought peanuts, Life Savers and a plain Hershey Bar.

He would go back to the ship now, catch up on all the news, read the funnies, do the puzzles, maybe even listen to the radio. Why not? It was Saturday night! So what if he was alone? He was alone before.

***

Four point four light years away, on planet Earth, a craggy-faced newsy in a tweed cap, tucked inside his newsstand and the lonely night on Fort Washington Avenue, under a flickering yellow light, awaited his last few customers for the remaining late edition papers. But in

155

his heart, he had long tired of the same faces, the familiar amenities, the well-worn exchanges. Beyond the visor of his cap, his tired eyes turned toward the night sky and the stars and galaxies afar, deep within it. His vision created alien craft soaring out from the heavens, settling before his earthly establishment and dispatching a dashing spaceman toward him. Certainly, he mused, the stranger and his companions aboard should like to read of all the earthly news, perhaps enjoy the magazines. And so, to the spaceman he would casually say, in a most unruffled manner: "Paper, mister?"

But there was no ship or spaceman, no customers at all at this hour; no one to hear him mutter as he had so many times to himself, with each passing shadow, "Paper?"

Lonely here, thought the old newsy huddled under yellow light with his night phantoms, but, he pondered as he turned his gaze to the stars in the dark, it's lonelier up there, I'll bet. Lonelier up there.

Super

There were times when I felt more alone than anyone I knew. I was too young to understand or appreciate real friendship, too young to have what the great psychologist Harry Stack Sullivan called the all-important chum of adolescence. The sole criterion, for me, in determining my aloneness was in being an only child. And adding to the sad feeling which prevailed at times was a sense of deprivation. Everyone I knew had one or more siblings; an older brother, a younger sister, a twin. When the sun went down, when play time was over and we were called in, pretty much everyone went home with someone, or to someone, with whom to continue the noise and frolic of the day. But I was alone.

But was I? I had a chum, a buddy, a pal. Square-jawed, sharp-featured, fearless and good-looking, he was like an older brother, a hero, whose exploits I followed carefully, whose subtle moves I sought to emulate. He wore a green hat, sported a yellow topper, was beyond fault, and was the undisputed paragon; a champion for the straight, the strong. He was Dick Tracy.

Now, Tracy and I went back to the days before he and his cases made the front page of the Sunday comic supplement, back in the mid-forties. I remember Tracy before his adventures were preceded by the now mandatory Crime Stoppers heading. He and I were pals before Tess Trueheart became his wife, before B.O. Plenty even met Gravel Gertie, from the early days of Pruneface, Flattop, and The Brow. I can remember some of those horrific, graphic stories before I could read, when the pictures of murder and mayhem, death and evildoers told all, before a comics code; and I loved it. We all relished the triumph of right over villains most wicked. We were not dissuaded by the gruesome. We were not squeamish. Tracy was in charge and could not fail.

My mother, who, in the early days before my reading skills were honed, served as guide through the weekly Tracy episodes and occasionally hinted of times past, alluding to old cases and adventures which were battled and resolved before I even lived. These old adventures and exploits held great fascination and mystery for me.

But Dick Tracy, I was to learn, lived not only on the Sunday pages of the newspapers. I found him, unexpectedly, one afternoon, on the cover of a strange comic book I had obtained in a trade. (Comic books were obtained primarily in one of two ways…if you don't count finding them, which almost never occurred: you either bought or traded them.)

The neighborhood stores, from which you bought, were serviced pretty much by one distributor, and that distributor carried the same line of books and magazines for all the outlets on his route. Some dealers may have objected to displaying certain issues, but for the most part, what you found in one neighborhood store or newsstand, you found in most other local outlets as well.

Comic books were a kind of window on the world for a kid; addressing a kid's perspective, they dealt with war, adventure, romance, crime, school, ethics, urban life, rural life, heroism. But if you visited another borough, or moved to a new area (which had a different distributor) you got a fresh perspective. Except for a few nearly universally sold titles such as *Superman, Batman, Archie,* and *Walt Disney Comics,* you might have been shocked to discover an entire rack of hitherto unexplored books, subjects, artwork, and heroes. The rack would seem to have been stocked from another world. The experience would render the day's new turf all the more alien, leaving the afternoon and the visit all the more strange and memorable. Apparently the kid from whom I got the startling Dick Tracy comic book had obtained it from another neighborhood. I had never seen anything like it before.

The name of the book was *Super Comics.* Dick Tracy was pictured on the cover in blazing color. I could hardly fathom Tracy on the cover of a comic book. What was he doing there? His size was impressive. A kid measures size differently than an adult. He doesn't perceive things so much as what they represent, but more in line with how they are actually shown; their size as they are drawn. Tracy's figure and face on the comic book cover seemed bigger, more lifelike. But more staggering was the revelation that Dick Tracy dwelt elsewhere and was reachable now through this other venue. I had thought he lived only on Sundays in the

New York Daily News. But here was another window. I was now privy to a new line on Dick Tracy.

I was so overcome and perplexed at this find that I, silently reading the cover to myself, pronounced it as "supper" comics, a title I justified as denoting a comic book to be read either during or after supper. To me then, it became even more enticing and dark; an evening, a night book!

That first night, (after supper) I read the opening Dick Tracy yarn. Tracy and his trusty partner Pat Patton (before he became chief) were investigating a bootleg tire ring and somehow got snared by the arch-criminal B-B Eyes. The detectives were forced to climb into a couple of cylinders which served as molds, and into which hot paraffin was poured. Immobilized in the wax, after the molds were broken to make the prisoners "easier to handle," Tracy and Patton were left alone in the abandoned warehouse. How will they free themselves and escape? I turned the page. TO BE CONTINUED.

Another thing I had never encountered! Up until then, my life had been an orderly series of beginnings and endings, openings and closings. What did they mean: "TO BE CONTINUED"? When? Where? I desperately turned pages hoping for the "continuation" to be close by. It was not. My search was only about to begin.

Perhaps it was mispronunciation of the book's title that hampered my initial search. No one had ever heard of "supper" comics. But I scanned racks, shelves, and counters with no luck as well. My neighborhood simply was not serviced by a *Super Comics* distributor. And, of course, the kid from whose stack of books I had traded had no idea where he had obtained the issue. Several months went by. Tracy and Patton were probably goners.

One memorable Friday evening, my parents and I were strolling through the 181st Street five-and-dime, better known as F.W. Woolworth. There was one counter, near one of the exits, laid out with hundreds of comic books, under glass. One of these books was often my reward for making the Woolworth trek quietly. And there it was. The logo had changed, the type was not as bold, and of course the cover was different. But it was what I had been seeking all these months: *Super Comics*. Oasis! Serendipity! And there was Tracy, resplendent on the cover of issue number 102, diving off a police launch after what appeared to be a drowning man. I was paralyzed with emotion. Speechless. And for a dime, promptly obtained, all the answers to the little mysteries of my life would soon be uncovered.

Of course, Tracy was fine, having long ago escaped from the abandoned garage and ridding himself of his paraffin shell. But how had that been accomplished? This latest issue of *Super Comics* bore no clues, for it was far more current than the one I had sought. Tracy was well on his way to newer difficulties, enmeshed in more modern adventures. The *Super* issue, which carried the answers I had hoped to find, which revealed just how Tracy's dilemma was resolved was lost. Anyway, that's the way I remembered it.

For the next fifty years, I carried the question of Tracy's escape with me, and pursued in the search for the mysterious issue which held the answer. But not only was that particular issue nearly impossible to unearth, I was unhappily learning that *Super Comics* were relatively scarce, indeed few dealers and collectors had ever heard of the title. I was beginning to think perhaps it was pronounced Supper. Enter Larry Doucet.

Larry Doucet was probably the foremost collector of Dick Tracy memorabilia in the United States, if not the world. He began his quest as a boy down south, riding his bike from candy store to candy store, hot on the heels of the great sleuth. And now he possessed just about everything related to the comic detective, from the most esoteric trivia to glorious original artwork and correspondence with the Gould family. He had written books on the subject, and was its undisputed authority, perhaps only lacking in hours beside Tracy in the squad car.

I knew Larry's name from his countless ads in antiques and collectibles journals over the years: "Anything Dick Tracy," the ad cried out. The request was followed by his name and address. So when I decided to divest myself of the few Tracy collectibles I owned, I knew where to turn. Of course, Larry already had captured mint condition examples of the items I offered, but our phone conversations and the common interests we shared began a long friendship beyond the bounds of the Tracy trance.

Early on, Larry and his wife Patricia invited my wife Rose Ann and me to their home. It was then I was introduced to The Collection: multiple rooms of Dick Tracy stuff, shiny, colorful, with items under glass, framed, in display cases, in plastic, on shelves; buttons, badges, games, and toys. There were items you had sought, items you suddenly recalled, and items you never even knew existed. It was impressive. I told Larry that one night he would enter the room to actually discover a six-foot, real-life Dick Tracy, complete with hat and coat, patiently waiting in the center of the room, ready to surrender to the collection. The real Dick Tracy seemed to be the only piece that was missing. And I wasn't too sure about that. Larry nodded, and we ate.

It was after dinner that I posed my life-long Super Tracy conundrum to my host. Larry rose, ducked around a bend, and emerged carrying a large box more than two and a half feet in length. In it was pretty much the entire collection of *Super Comics,* in as near mint condition as age would allow. They were in cellophane protective covers backed by cardboard supports. "Go ahead," he said, "look through them." I glanced at the jackets through the cellophane, carefully. For the first time, I saw what about fifteen years of this elusive item looked like, many of Tracy's cases and adventures encapsulated on the enticing covers. Several drawn, written, read before I was born. Almost none of which had I ever seen.

Over the next few months, Larry shared some of his contacts with me and helped me obtain a nifty, albeit pricey, collection of Supers, as we referred to them. Altogether, I managed, over the months, to amass some fifty separate issues. One of the last I bid on, and won, was the memorable number 102. Receiving it was thrilling. It nearly brought back that fall Friday night at the Woolworth when the bright blue and black cover first met my eye, and for a moment I felt a kind of retread of that initial joy. I was not especially anxious to read the story inside, and as most collectors do with their trophies, I simply put it away. I would have been more excited to find the issue which explained how Tracy and Patton escaped from their paraffin cylinders. But I had not, however, even identified in which Super that story was printed. The answer to the fifty-year-old mystery of how they made good their escape would lie somewhere between that issue and number 102.

When I had accumulated what I thought was a sufficient number of Super issues that preceded 102, I began looking for the story I thought I had remembered so well. I couldn't find it. In none of the magazines were the detectives trapped in an abandoned garage warehousing tires. What was going on? I decided to open number 102, but only to reacquaint myself with Tracy's more recent adventure, the one that followed on the heels of the tire caper. It hadn't followed. It <u>was</u> the tire affair; paraffin cylinders and all. And it was pretty much complete too, showing how Tracy and Patton moved their feet to throw their confined selves to the floor, breaking the molds. Somehow, apparently, it was the story in 102 that had impressed me over the years. 102 was not the disappointment I had thought it to be; it had been the source of the whole fantasy. But then…what was the saga "to be continued" that impelled me to pursue the next issue of Super Comics, which as it happened, turned out to be number 102? What story, what forgotten Tracy dilemma was that? In which issue was that secreted? I couldn't even recall what that cover might have looked like. I glanced through color copies of Super covers I had known to exist. Larry had made them for me. Nothing rang a bell. The puzzle, it seemed, although in slightly different form, remained.

And on days when afternoons are quiet and things settle into a less-than-exciting mode, when not too many new packages are left to open, I take down the binders. When little looms on more serious horizons, I stare at the crisp Supers, at the colorful covers that journeyed through the years, I relish the images beneath the clear plastic, and ponder the tales that lie within, and I flip to the issues between 90 and 102, for surely the answer to my enigma lies somewhere here. I savor that thought. But I no longer look. I have already had my chance. Time and memory play strange tricks. I am still missing some Super issues and perhaps the answer is therein. I will check someday. Maybe. But for now, the mystery, happily, remains.

The Birthday Card

Recently, my old friend Ross had a birthday. We had exchanged a few cards over the years, some of which evoked a chuckle. The greeting I had sent prior to the last one proved so hilarious, topping it became a challenge. Store-bought card humor was now out of the question. In any case, when you get right down to it, birthdays are not all that amusing anymore. But it being impingent upon me to commemorate the date of old Ross's special day, not wishing to cede to defeat, I came up with the following, after a somewhat extended period of thought. I include it herein as a greeting to all of you readers, particularly those of you who spent the first ten years of your lives between 1940 and 1950 or so in Washington Heights. The card read:

HAPPY BIRTHDAY!

THE WHOLE GANG SAYS HI!

Noah Hardy

Jon Hardy

Rudy Hirscheimer

Ralph Bernheimer

Richard Feare

Marshall Zulo

Jerry Pollizzi

Alan Koppel

Steven Olendorf

Robert Freed

Robert Paulive

Don Baylek

Alfred Feldman

Ward Roban

James Corrides

Enrique Chaffarday

Emilio Mejia

Joseph Finger

John Sturka

Richie Martell

Charles Littman

Eleanor Littman

Ellen Price

Ellen Plant

Joan Miller

Ross Fishman

Bernard Bacharach

Gary Birnbaum

Malcolm Burke

Rhoda Burke

Jack Goldman

Jay Alper

Carmen Salgado

Maryann Tormos

Joyce Roth

Harriet Simms

Charlie Rothchild

Robert Rothstien

Ronald Ettus

Jacob Rosen

Levy Laub

George Heral

Tommy Worms

Johnny Worms

Claus Wolfe
Joseph Goldman
Raymond Curry
Lawrence Friedland
Billy Jones
Russell Breer
Mary Hopkins
Evelyn Strolberg
Joan Bettauer
Walter Sirota
Walter Mussliner
Loretta Blum
Lillian Meletz
Edward Gaynor
Gus Minetos
Pete Minetos
Stathy Minetos
George Fondotas
Ralph Weil
Spencer Beleah
Kenneth Pierce
Joel Marcuse

Nancy Solomon
Joan Gotis
Robert Winkler
Doris Wagner
Doris Mayer
Jon Mayer
Leon Heller
Pete Psirogianes
Kenneth Stern
David Peltz
Eddie Hupschmidt
Arnie Alperin
Lewis Alperin
George Levitt
Dorothy Channin
Alice Platt
Judy Leopold
David Krieger
Red Thompson
Kathleen Armatage
Tommy Armatage
Henry Ramer

Linda Winton
Paul Winton
Harvey Janoff
Judith Sonnenberg
Adrian Scholnik
Michael Scholnik
Anastasia Lazos
Kenny Munchein
Jacqueline Jacobson
Rosalind Harris
Mark Trout
Manny Dominquez
Carol Fischer
Ann Nachman
Carol Metz
Betsy Rosenbloom
Alan Cass
Marcia Reisman
Ruby Sulkes
Ruth Gordon
Betty Perera
Rosemary Gillis

Richard Zimmer
Howard Siegler
Arlene Siegler
Kenneth Fitzgerald
Alan Bischoff
William Wilkerson
Herbert Semel
George Brady
Eugene Rosenbaum
Ivan Haskell
Sanya Rosner
Penny Collis
Jackie Roe
Billy Simon
Jerry Thomas
Alex Larys
Rodger Malera
Chubby Vacaroles
Bobby Luckinbach
Arthur Luckinbach
Stephen Josias
Harvey Raines

Richard Dolan
Mickey Epstein
Ruben Sitchel Stern
Arnold Nager
Robert Farber
Robert Brophe
Ronald Woods
Michael Dreslin
Bobby Stewart
Winston Stewart
Lionel Baumed
Philip Fogarty
Betty Fogarty
Judy Lumley
Jerry Nusbaum
George Bustamante
Harvey Raines
Roger Halpern
Melvin Arnold
Arnold Burke
Toby Burke
Freddy Comes

Robert Smiley
Michael Cole
Larry Cole
Westley Zion
Bill Lubliner
Eddie Gallison
Ralph Guerra
Marty Jacobs
Phyllis Landau
Margo Rosenheimer
Hilde Rosenheimer
Peter Ottensauser
Larry Loeb
Lenny Maltin
Jerome Albenberg
Billy O'Brian
Al Blaustien
Marty Kornreich
Jack Kornreich
Steve Borrow
Artie Fleischer
Ronald Fogel

Joe Pargament
Fran Pargament
Nicole
Alba
Frenchy
Benny
Suzanne
Peter
Emily
Kenny
Illana
Evelyn
Jeff
Sid

Teachers-<u>P. S. 173</u>
Mrs.Caroll
Mrs. Callinan
Mrs. Columbia
Mrs. Eigan
Mrs. Goldman
Mrs. Navazio

Mrs. Hamm
Mrs. Seligman
Mrs. McCormack
Mrs. Bouton
Miss Hannan
Mrs. Critchley
Mrs. Flynn
Mrs. Weisman
Mrs. Martin
Mrs. Hart
Miss Duffy
Mrs. Driscoll
Mrs. Storm
Mrs. Mandell
Miss Ferguson
Mrs. O'Neill
Mrs. Levine
Mrs. Bayer
Mrs. Handel
Mr. Peters
Mr. Wolf
Miss Lewis

Mrs. Hines
Brad

JHS 115-Teachers
Mr. Press
Mr. Presioso
Mr. DeWit
Mrs. Kiernan
Mrs. Moore
Mrs. Roberts
Mr. Metzelar
Miss Clemens
Miss Moraines
Miss Wolan
Miss Whelan
Mr. Seaman
Mrs. Geist
Mr. Knowlson
Mr. Banks

Gary

One Last Word
(Or so…)

And remember… Getty's Drugstore and the Sportsman's Colognes in the window around Christmastime; with the jumping trout and the drake on the square bottles; Daitch Dairy; Humpty Dumpty Children's Shop; Welo Camera; Spritzer's German Restaurant near Loewe's?

Remember…Valle Pastry; The Pennysaver; The many candy stores that were signed as everything but? Rosse and Sobol (Harry and Dave's); Stern's Stationery (Dave's) and Dave's two brothers, and Pop, who sat outside on Broadway in the early forties with his vest and Derby hat; Lesnick's; Gaynor's; and Mintz's? And on the east side of Broadway, Jack and Charlie, neither of whom ever smiled, and hated the kids who pestered them, and who made you wonder why they were in the candy store business in the first place.

Ascot Drugs; The White Star Market; Benny's pickles and sauerkraut in the barrel; The Silver Palm, one of the "newer," more modern, restaurants in the neighborhood; the Furrier with the stuffed young polar bear in the window; The China View Restaurant; The Broadway Delicatessen with the two gray-jacketed waiters, the one with the deep furrows in his face and Max, forever shouting "Two Frranks Vitt!" to the counterman. A roast beef sandwich, FF Pot, and a Dr. Brown Cel-Ray was 90 cents with a dime left for the tip.

And there was the Sunshine Dairy, Rappaport Fish and Zeitlin Drugs, with that Ex-Lax tin thermometer hanging outside the entrance for what seemed like forever. There was Maxim's Bakery, The Isaac Gelis Deli, and across the street, Morris' Meats. Farther to the south, there was the wonderful Gene's Bookshop, Mac's Appetizing, Riverside Pastry, and Levine's Fruits. (Mac's sold little chocolate jelly-filled candies in red and blue cellophane wrappers, the likes of which I never tasted nor did I ever see again.)

There were banks. The Harlem Savings and the Corn Exchange Bank; Indian Walk Shoes, and Volland Florists. And the hat stores: Vogue Hats, Young Hats, Adam Hats, and Bettina Hats. And remember the Charlotte Russe? Looked better than it tasted...little bit of sponge cake topped with whipped cream and a cherry in a white cardboard holder. Sometimes the cake part would fall through....

The Automat, of course, was the heart of east 181st Street, but the real treat was the Horn and Hardart takeout retail shop, where you could actually bring home the baked beans, the spaghetti, and the creamed spinach. And the clothing stores for men: Crawford, Bond, Ripley, and the "newly opened" Howard. And the pipe store, and the stamp store, Fanny Farmer, before it became Cinderella's, and the other real candy stores: Loft, Gardner's, Barton's, and Barricini.

There was Walsh's Bar and Grill and that bar on Broadway where they said Buster shot himself to death playing Russian roulette.

These were the stations along the way; the places of sorrow and joy, of tastes, touches, and scents where we won and lost, and watched the seasons pass. These are the markers of memories in the rain and the sun, with family and friends. Now, on our evening's trip, these were...this was...The Heights we can still remember.

ON BWY LOOKING TOWARD 181st STREET

ON 181st STREET AT WADSWORTH AVENUE

"MOM AND DAD ON 178th STREET"

Epilogue: 132

132 was invariably surrounded, for me, by an aura of mystery. My image of it was cold, gray, sterile and unfriendly, although this was unfair to say the least. Not only had I not attended the school, I had never even seen the place. And, just for the record, it is P.S. 132; but I never heard it referred to as that. It was simply 132.

Despite my image, and on whatever reasons it may have been founded, three of the sweetest girls I had ever known emerged from that school. This is worth noting because it is my impression that, as a child, aliens are determined by a few factors, one of which is attending another school. It is as if those going to that school emit a strange glow, partake in secret rituals, and themselves keep strange company, about which we know nothing. We perceive those being educated in other institutions as different; not so much a part of us as those with whom we share common teachers, classrooms, instruction. Perhaps we fear a breach at some fundamental level of communication. But meeting and coming to know

Marcia, Ruby, and Harriet of 132 dispelled most of that, insofar as those girls were concerned, anyway.

This trio of young ladies played ping-pong with us at a common recreation place, the Y, after our respective schools let out. Marcia later appeared, a year my senior, in the high school I attended (not a neighborhood school) and some decades later, her picture came to my attention in an older friend's yearbook. During college, I knew this small 132 group, along with others who lived north of 181st Street, congregated at a place called Al's Diner, farther up along Broadway, but somehow I failed to immerse myself in that clique; showing up only once or twice with Cabrini Boulevard pals to squeeze in at a table for a burger and coffee. By this stage in our lives, I should mention, receiving or having received education in other schools was forgiven, and those recipients were not disparaged nor seen as alien. Still, however, I never quite embraced 132, nor put it on par with my first alma mater, P.S. 173.

To digress for a moment, my father, an advertising representative for magazines, was never without two pocket-sized paper books he carried and frequently consulted. One of these was a diary/appointment affair filled with his scrawl, noting people, places, times, dates, and events. The other, which always fascinated me, was far more interesting. It came packed with pre-printed material in tiny letters and numbers, revealing lists, maps, regulations and instructions. It bore pages of information on bus and subway routes, trolley and elevated lines, street and house numbers, and notes on bridges, tunnels, railroads, and places of interest. It was called the Red Book, oddly, because its ornately lettered cover was a drab brown. But inside this little 200-pager you could find the locations of hotels, police stations, post offices, and theaters. You might discover libraries, clubs, office buildings, and fraternal orders. From steamboat lines to skating rinks, from markets to museums, with the Red Book, you could find your way around.

When my father died, I discovered the Red Book among his papers and cherished possessions. Going through it and carefully reading the pages was like embarking on a trip back into and through the 1940s. Now, more than half of the department stores were gone; the banks were mostly transformed or had vanished; "amusement resorts," "airplane fields," "air mail routes"? "Comfort stations," "bath houses," "homes and asylums"? What were these? The city had changed radically.

As I leafed through the Red Book's contents, it occurred to me not only had I never seen P.S.132, I did not know on what street it stood. P.S.173 was on 173rd Street, P.S. 189 was on 189th Street. Where did that leave 132? I looked it up. 185 Wadsworth Avenue. And where was that? I turned in the book to Wadsworth Avenue. 185 was between 182nd and 183rd Street. I felt a surge of enlightenment, learning something that for the last sixty years I had not known nor thought about. 132 had been one of those alien places, out there, somewhere on the fringes of Washington Heights. But now that I knew precisely where it stood, now that I possessed the knowledge of where Ruby and Marcia and Harriet had come from, where their lives began, I wanted to experience the place for myself; at least to see it.

I did not travel back to Washington Heights right away, but savored the idea of the trip, the adventure. The day did come, however, after completing this series of tales which had its genesis in Washington Heights. I thought I owed the jaunt back to that particular corner of time and space to my readers and to myself. Incidentally, I say "time," perhaps not so much "space," because for me that's what it was. Much of the "space" had undergone transformation, but what configuration remained constant brought me back through time to that long gone place.

The number 4 bus ride was uneventful. Up Madison Avenue, across 110th and Cathedral Parkway, then north on Broadway and finally Fort Washington Avenue. I passed 173, J. Hood Wright Park and the Bridge, and got off at 181st Street. Pretty much everything was gone or changed, but I was surprised at how much I felt the same as I had on many a bright day walking along that very path, years ago. The place was teeming with activity. It was not as dark as I had imagined. The summer blazed through the August afternoon. The sun showed gold on everything. It was as cheerful a midday as I can ever recall and the heat was not oppressive. The trail was a montage of motion although no one seemed to be going anywhere. Everyone on 181st Street appeared to be wringing what they could from the bustling hours. The colors were more intense than the noises I could hear. Brilliance outshone sound. Almost in slow motion, I made my way through the mosaic to Wadsworth Avenue and turned north to 182nd Street.

And there it was. P.S. 132. I had never been here. I had, foolishly, never seen it.

The sadness I felt at that was enveloping.

Turning onto Wadsworth Avenue in itself was unsettling. The street was quiet, nearly deserted, certainly, compared to the main thoroughfare of 181st Street. The summer was still upon us, so the school was closed. I took a few pictures and stood there. Looking up at the school, I found it to be less imposing than it had been in my mind all these years, and I wondered what it was like in 1945. Probably not so different than now.

Then I realized, in two weeks or so, as a fresh school term begins, a whole new crop of Marcias and Marias, Marcs and Marianos, will converge here once again. They will serve their time; meet up with their counterparts from down the road at 173. They will summer in the park, play on the ball field, and eventually rendezvous at Al's Diner or some similar coffee loitering hole, as 132, again, becomes a memory. They will do it all again, just as we did. And that's what counts. Because that's all there is.

And, in about sixty years, say 2065, some dude'll stop by, stand at this very spot, and wonder: whatever happened to yesterday?

"132 TODAY"

George Washington Bridge, New York

About the Author

Gary Alexander Azerier has been a New York Broadcaster since 1964, where he was heard on WINS, WCBS and the NBC network, after serving as a Radio Correspondent for the Second Division of the U.S. Marine Corps. He was raised in Washington Heights and educated in New York City, where he currently resides with his wife Rose Ann.

Printed in the United States
75107LV00001B/60